To The Cache La Poudre
(Buckskin Chronicles 7)

B. N. Rundell

To The Cache La Poudre
(Buckskin Chronicles 7)

B. N. Rundell

WOLFPACK
PUBLISHING
— EST 2013 —

Wolfpack Publishing
6032 Wheat Penny Avenue
Las Vegas, NV 89122

This book is a work of fiction. Any references to historical events, real people or real places are used fictitiously. Other names, characters, places and events are products of the author's imagination, and any resemblance to actual events, places or persons, living or dead, is entirely coincidental.

Print Edition ISBN 978-1-62918-758-7

Dedication

To dedicate a work of time, effort and love is to say that those moments of time and the exercise of effort and the love expended were given as a gift to another. And yet the other to whom I would give that gift is really the other part of me, and she is my better half and my partner for life, my wife, Dawn, who has been my partner these past fifty-one years. But this is not a solitary work, for to make a dream or vision become a reality requires more than time, effort, love and assistance. There are many minds and hands and hearts that combine to make this work a reality and some may never know what they have contributed. It might have been a kind word, and expression of encouragement, or even a written paragraph by someone in the distant past, but all combined to make this a reality. And to each and every one I say thank you.

Chapter One

Departure

THE MORNING SUN was framed with the broad brush of orange clouds that spread their wings across the Eastern ridge of the Medicine Bow Mountains. The warmth was welcome on the face of Talon Thompsett as he ushered the small herd of cross-bred cattle up the trail alongside the south bank of Camp Creek. A mottled grey dog worried the heels of the lagging steers that weren't happy with the young man's choice of trails and they repeatedly kicked at the scampering dog to show their disapproval. This wasn't the first time that Talon had used this trail to cross this stretch of mountains, but it was the first time anyone had dared to take cattle through the black timber that shouldered the trail.

Spring came early this year and the trail through the mountains was mostly clear of snow, but the northern slopes and shady areas still harbored drifts that hampered progress and the cattle didn't like anything about busting snowdrifts. When Talon's well-trained dog, Smokey, took after the laggards, the drifts became the lesser of two evils and the trail was soon made through the hazards. Talon wanted to clear the timber on the east side before making camp for the night and they still had a-ways to go, but there were only a couple of hours of daylight left.

Several times, his dusty-colored Grulla mustang-bred gelding would bump up against the rump of the slower moving steers and push them up the trail. There was very little that would keep his horse from moving the cattle on the trail, for this horse and Talon had practically been raised together. Talon was just nine-years-old when his dad, Caleb, had presented him and his twin brother, Tyrell, with horses for their birthdays. Talon's was a Grulla gelding he had admired since it was born just two years earlier, and Tyrell's was a line-back dun mare of the same age. Although the boys had worked with horses since they were big enough to walk on their own, this was the first time they did all the training and breaking of their own mounts.

Talon had relished the idea of making his horse not just a cow horse, but a true mountain horse and his Grulla, Dusty, had fulfilled his dream. Now, they were on their own and pushing this small herd across the mountains and down to Camp Collins. With the two most difficult days behind them, four more days would see the trip complete, but now it was time to look for a camp for the night.

After breaking clear of the timber, the wide meadow between the tall pines and the west bank of the Laramie River served as a natural holding area for the small herd. It was a well-chosen site for camp as dusk replaced the bright afternoon sunlight. As the cattle settled down to graze and rest up after their day-long climb over the mountains, Talon de-rigged his mount and pack horse to prepare camp and coffee. A simple meal of left-over corn pone and fresh grilled venison steak washed down by hot, black coffee gave the young man a satisfying end to the long day. He leaned back against a grey log and stared at the glowing embers of the dying fire and relived the last several days that had brought him to this place.

The twins, Tyrell and Talon, had, as most twins do, spent their lives in competition in everything. When the big former stevedore, Reuben, taught them some of the moves of riverfront fighting, they practiced on each other. As Spotted Owl schooled them in the art of hunting with a bow and arrow, they sought to outdo one another with game bagged. As Caleb and Clancy shared their knowledge of the wilderness and game calls and tracking, they would chase one another through the woods. And as the Bible teaches, "Iron sharpeneth Iron," both the young men grew in knowledge and skill and mastered the ways of the wilderness at an early age.

Both were beyond measure in their mastery of marksmanship with rifle, pistol and bow. They were equally adept with tomahawk and knife as well as Indian-style hand to hand fighting, with the added skills of waterfront free-for-all fisticuffs and wrestling.

The boys had grown to the size of men with broad shoulders, lean frames and well developed muscles. Their dark red hair and freckled complexions turned even darker with the summer sun and the boys were often mistaken for mixed breed. Yet at fourteen, coming on fifteen, Talon had chosen to strike out on his own, after losing the one contest that mattered, that of winning the heart of Elizabeth, the daughter of Chance and Marylyn Threet, the beautiful blonde girl that both boys had wooed since they were old enough to even consider the opposite sex.

Talon and Tyrell were the only sons of Caleb and Clancy Thompsett, who had been raised by Jeremiah Thompsett and Laughing Waters of the Northern Arapaho in the Wind River Mountains. Caleb was the step son of Jeremiah's sister and had come west with Jeremiah when he was but nine-years-old, and it was about three years later that Clancy, who was the sole survivor of a Crow massacred wagon train, was taken in by the couple. When Caleb and Clancy started a ranch in the Medicine Bow valley, they were blessed with twins and the family grew together on the first ranch in the wilderness. The

3

twins benefited from the education of the varied backgrounds of the family and friends in the valley. Now, Talon had chosen to strike off on his own and find his way in the fast-changing world of the west.

As was his habit, he greeted the rising sun from the back of his horse as he pushed the small herd across the shallows of the Laramie River. It was an easy crossing and made without incident with the cows bellowing their belligerence as soon as they struck dry ground on the east bank. Almost a year before, Talon and his dad and brother made a similar drive of a larger herd of cattle, but they had taken a longer route by going north and east of the Medicine Bow Range before swinging south along the Overland Trail.

Talon chose to use what he thought would be a shorter route and he was pleased with himself to have made the drive across the shorter trail. He knew he had saved at least three days of travel and he was already looking forward to reaching his destination of Camp Collins at the mouth of the Cache La Poudre Canyon.

With the Laramie River at his back, he pushed the herd east through the flats, keeping the taller timber to his south with the grassy meadows before him until the valley opened along the Overland Trail. He would run parallel to the east branch of the Cherokee Trail until he reached LaPorte. With his dog, Smokey, as his only helper, he was certain he could make the remainder of the drive in no more than four days and maybe, with luck, as little as three days.

Talon was well-outfitted for his journey, with most of the gear on the pack horse that included his bedroll, cooking utensils and other supplies, as well as, a well-crafted ash and cherry wood bow and a good supply of steel tipped arrows. Under his right leg was a scabbard that carried the big bore .56-.56 Spencer repeater while another scabbard in front of his left leg harbored his .44 Henry repeater. He preferred having both rifles with the Spencer serving the purpose for the bigger game such as buffalo and bear, but the easy-to-handle Henry was perfect for most other purposes.

He also sported a new Model Remington Army revolver in .44 caliber in a holster on his left hip with the butt forward and canted toward his right hand, two additional loaded cylinders were nestled in separate pouches on his belt to the far left of the holster. Tucked into the right side of his beaded belt was a well-used but very sharp tomahawk and hanging between his shoulder blades and completely out of sight was a razor-sharp Bowie knife.

By any standards, Talon would be considered expert with any and all of the weapons, but none were on display and all were rather inconspicuously carried. Time and again, Talon had proven his expertise at bringing the weapons into play within seconds as need required. He was very comfortable with the weapons and gave little thought to them as they were as much a part of his regular attire as were the moccasins on his feet. His attire was a complete set of well-made and simply adorned buckskins, lovingly crafted by his mother who had been taught by her mother, the Shaman of the Arapaho people. A broad-brimmed, dark brown felt hat protected his head and completed his outfit. First glance at the young man would be deceiving to anyone as his demeanor and attire was that of a mature man and not that of the youth that he was, but his maturity was well beyond his years.

Mid-morning of the fourth day, Talon pushed the cattle to skirt the north edge of the growing town of LaPorte and onto the trail that would take them to Camp Collins. Nearing the post, he moved the cattle to a small meadow-like area at the edge of the bluff where they would circle up and graze to be held in place by the dog until his business could be finished with the post commander. When Talon was ushered into the commander's office, he introduced himself, "Morning Lieutenant, I'm Talon Thompsett. My dad and I brought some cattle down here last year and were told that if we brought more, you and your troops would be happy to have them."

"Pleasure to meet you, Mr. Thompsett, I'm Lieutenant George Hawkins, and yes, we will be happy to take them off your hands. A good beef steak will be a welcome change from the venison we've been eating all winter. How many did you bring us?"

"I've got twenty head circled up out yonder by the trees."

"O.K., well, the last time I was down in Denver City, they were paying $25 per head, but with the continuing gold rush and growing demand, they say the price had gone up, so how does $30 per head sound?"

"Well, that sounds fine, Lieutenant. However, I would prefer payment in gold coin, if that's suitable with you?"

"I think we can accommodate you with that, course it'll probably take most of the coin I have on hand, but I'm sure we can do that."

The Lieutenant turned from his desk to a small safe behind him, retrieved a tray with the money, and counted out thirty, twenty-dollar gold pieces for Talon. The young man smiled as he stood and dropped the coin into a leather draw-string pouch, shook the Lieutenant's hand and turned to leave. "Do you want me to leave the cattle there, or do you need them moved somewhere else?"

"No, I'll get my men to move them to the meadow behind the fort. It's a well-protected area and they'll have grass to eat before we turn them into steak." The lieutenant smiled as he thought of the savory steak he and his men would soon share. With a slight wave, he bid good bye to Talon.

The young man sauntered to his mount and rode back toward town in anticipation of a good meal and a comfortable night in a hotel. On the way, he turned off the trail and made his way into the trees. Finding a secluded spot, he dismounted, tied off his mount and the pack horse and began to secure his newly acquired coin.

Chapter Two

LaPorte

HIS FIRST VISIT to the growing town of LaPorte was with his Dad the year before and little time was spent in the town. They made a quick trip to deliver the cattle and turned right around to head back to the ranch, but now he had plenty of time to explore the town. Stopping at the livery, he secured a stall for his horses and asked the resident smithy, "Ya got any place for me to store my gear?"

"Shore do, there be a tack room yonder, we lock it up ever night, but if you got sumpin' real valuable, you might wanna keep it witchu, cuz if'n sombuddy really wanted in thar, that piddlin' little lock ain't gonna keep 'em out."

"Well, I just want ta' keep my gear reasonably safe, ain't worth much, just a saddle an' pack saddle an' stuff, so I'm guessin' it'll be alright in thar'," drawled Talon as he began unsaddling Dusty and turned him into the stall for a bit of grain. After de-rigging the pack horse and putting him into his own stall, Talon carried the saddles and gear into the tack room and hung it on the pegs and hangers. Keeping his Henry and

7

scabbard and his saddle bags, he asked the smithy, "Where can
I get a place to stay an' somethin' to eat?"

"Well, depends… if yore hungry an' thirsty, then go to the
Four Aces saloon, they got purty good grub and the drinks ain't
too watered down. But if you want a place to sleep and some
good food, go to Auntie Stone's. She's got a little hotel and she
puts out the best food in town, but she don't have no likker."

"And where's this Auntie Stone's?"

"Down there at the end of the street, just 'fore ya git to the
river. If ya git to the bridge, ya done gone too fer."

Talon nodded his head in thanks to the smithy, and with
his saddle bags on his left shoulder and his Henry in his right
hand he started down the boardwalk toward the hotel. It was a
casual stroll as he took in the sights of the bustling town that
had become quite the supply center for emigrants. He had
noted a wagon train circled up on the edge of town when he
came through that morning and as the smithy explained, that
would just be the first of many for the coming summer.
Several folks were crowding the boardwalk and moving in and
out of the few businesses.

The biggest crowd was just in front of Talon as they made
their way into the largest building which housed the thriving
general store. This would be where many from the wagon train
would be re-supplying and the crowd acted as if they had to get
their supplies before they ran out, although the store was well
supplied and not in any danger of running short. Talon stepped
off the boardwalk and walked around the crowd, stepping back
up on the walkway just as a couple of young ladies broke from
the crowd amidst a gaggle of giggles and bumped into the over-
burdened young man.

"Oh, excuse us! We didn't see you there, Mr. . . ." said a
very attractive brunette that appeared to be about the same age
as Talon and was wearing a red and white checked gingham
dress and bonnet to match. Her friend was in a pale grey dress
and a white bonnet that covered long red tresses. Both girls
smiled from under slightly bowed brows.

Talon sat his Henry against a post that held up the second-floor veranda, doffed his hat to reveal his tousled dark red hair and said, "Thompsett, Miss, Talon Thompsett, at your service."

"Oh my, and a gentleman, even if you are in buckskins. I never thought we'd meet a gentleman out here in the wild West, did you, Ginny?" asked the girl in grey.

"Oh, don't be so brash, Mary Sue, he's just being mannerly. After all, we did bump into him, not the other way around." She looked at Talon and continued, "If you will excuse us, Mr. Thompsett, good day."

"And good day to you ladies, as well," he replied and watched them continue down the boardwalk. He smiled as he admired them and waited for them to look back. Within just a few seconds, they both tried to appear casual as they looked over their shoulders and caught him smiling at them. He tipped his hat and looked away, picked up his Henry and continued his way to the hotel. As he walked with Smokey at his heels, he passed others from the wagon train, as well as, several miners and some obvious residents. Like every town, there were those ne'er-do-wells that hung out on the streets and watched everyone else. Talon saw two men that had commandeered a couple of ladder back chairs from somewhere and were leaning back against the wall of the doctor's office as they observed the passers-by. Talon didn't hear the two as they nodded in his direction and spoke to one another. "Hey, ain't he the one we saw pushin' them cows up to the sojer boys?"

"Yeah, I think he is, leastways, he looks like the one we saw," answered the skinny one.

"Ya think he sold them cows to the sojers?" asked the one with a scraggly black beard.

"Must have, 'n if'n he did, I bet he got hisself a passel o' money."

"I wisht we had some cows to sell to them sojer boys."

"Don't need no cows, we'll just take the money off'n him."

The two men dropped the chairs down off the wall and stood to follow Talon.

9

The boardwalk took the young man past two saloons before arriving at the hotel. He pushed his way into the hotel lobby and walked to the desk where an older woman was busy with some dusting but she looked up with a smile and greeted Talon with, "Welcome, welcome. How can I help you?"

"Well, ma'am, I'm looking for a room for the night and the smithy said this was also the best place in town for puttin' on the feed bag. Was he right?"

She smiled broadly and answered, "Well, I like to think so, and yes, we do have a room available. Just one night?"

"I think so, I don't rightly know. I'm not sure what I'm goin' to be doin' come tomorrow, but I'll rope that steer when it comes so we'll just count on tonight for now, if that's alright."

"Of course, I'll get your key. You'll have the second room at the top of the stairs and we'll start serving dinner in just a little while."

"That'll be fine, ma'am. Thank you," replied Talon as he took the key and started for the stairs.

Across from the hotel stood a stage station where the two drifters took up their vigil. They weren't sure how they would do it, but they were determined to relieve the buckskin attired man of any money he received for delivering the cattle to Camp Collins. Of course, they had no idea how much money was involved, but they knew it was more than the four dollars they currently had between them. Since they'd gotten a good look at the buck-skinner and saw he was a young man, they thought it wouldn't be difficult to take down the youngster and easily enrich themselves, it was just a matter of waiting for him to come out and they would follow him and strike after dark. It should be easy, after all, they had done it several times before and to much bigger men. They tried to appear as if they were just waiting for a stage as they lounged about.

Auntie Stone served her meals family-style with everyone seated around a big, long table in the main dining room. It accommodated fourteen people with five on each side and two at each end and no meal saw empty chairs.

It was usual for Auntie Stone to empty the table two and three times per meal with everyone going away full and happy. Talon had the end seat on one side with four men on the same side, three men and two women on the opposite side and two couples at each end of the long table. The meal was fresh rainbow trout fried with cornmeal dressing, buttered asparagus, potatoes and rhubarb pie for desert. Everyone focused on the meal and little conversation was to be had. There were tidbits of introductions and gossip shared but little attention was paid to anything but the table-fare. As Talon pushed back with a steaming cup of black coffee, he smiled at his hostess, lifted his cup and mouthed the words, "Thank you", receiving a smile of thanks.

When he finished, he stood, picked up his hat and headed to the door anticipating an evening walk around the part of town he had yet to explore. Auntie Stone headed him off and said, "Your dog, Smokey, I think you said his name was, well, I've made a bed for him on the back porch just off the kitchen and he's helping me out by taking care of some of the table scraps, if that's alright with you?"

"He always did kinda take to the ladies, and yes, that's alright with me. If he gets to be too much of a bother, just turn him into my room and he'll make his bed on my gear and mind his manners."

"That'll be fine, I like dogs and he sure is a pretty one with those big blue eyes. I'm sure he'll be fine. You enjoy your walk around our town, now."

Talon tipped his hat and made his way to the door and quietly exited. Crossing the street, he bypassed the stage station and stepped onto the boardwalk in front of the Four Aces saloon. He strolled along as he peered into the windows of the saloon and saw the growing crowd of revelers with many at the tables partaking in games of chance and others standing at the bar downing their drinks of choice. A tin-pan piano banged out an unfamiliar tune but it didn't matter as no one paid any attention to the efforts of the semi-sober musician.

11

Next to the saloon was a brewery and Talon looked in the window at the busy workers still at their jobs amidst the large wooden casks. The activities of the night kept the young man almost oblivious to the many other people on the darkening streets.

"It's almost dark enough, but if we don't get him 'fore he goes back to the hotel, we might not get 'nother chance," observed Eli, the bearded attacker.

"Lookee here, you follow him, hang back a mite, an' I'll be behind the buildin's. When I get a chance, I'll sneak in 'tween a couple of 'em, and knock him on the head. You drag him into the alleyway, and we'll take the money an' skedaddle," ordered Albert, the skinny mastermind.

Talon continued his leisurely stroll and enjoyed the cool of the evening and the friendly folks that passed him by on the boardwalk. He stepped down from the walkway and crossed in front of the second blacksmith shop and livery and watched as sparks flew from the anvil and hammer of the smithy's work. Next to the smithy was a butcher shop that was closing for the evening and Talon spoke to the butcher as he locked his doors, "Evenin' sir, how's business been?"

"Well, not too bad. But folks have been gettin' tired of venison and been askin' for beef which I don't have."

"I just brought twenty head to Camp Collins, delivered 'em this mornin'," shared Talon.

"Wish I'da knowed that, I woulda taken some of 'em! It's mighty hard to get beef up here. Where'd you get the beef from?"

"My family has a ranch up in the Medicine Bow valley on the North Platte. I drove 'em down from there. Only took a week."

"Well, next time you want to bring down some, I'll sure buy 'em from you."

"I'll keep that in mind, although I don't expect to be doin' it anytime soon."

"Well, don't forget now, y'hear?"

Talon nodded his head and continued his stroll while the butcher continued his closing routine. Next to the butcher shop was another saloon, this one making four saloons for this small town. Talon shook his head in wonder at how such a small town could support so many saloons but he recalled seeing quite a few miners and, of course, the many wagon trains the smithy had told him about would provide several more, thirsty men to support the saloons.

He dawdled a bit in front of the windows as he watched three dancing women on a small stage trying to keep time with another tin-pan piano while several shouting men waved their hats in the air and hooted at the girls shaking their skirts to the entertainment of the men.

Dark had fallen and the only light on the streets was that from the windows of the still- open businesses. The moon was hidden behind a heavy cover of clouds and the stars were equally obscured, making the night as black as the depth of a hard-rock mine. Talon stepped off the end of the boardwalk and started to cross the street when he was struck on the back of the head causing him to crumple to the ground in the blackness of the night.

"Quick, drag him back in here!" came the hoarse whisper from Albert as he ordered Eli.

The big bearded man grabbed Talon under the armpits and drug him in the direction of the waiting Albert. He was almost behind the side wall of the saloon when he heard a shout, "Hey! You there! What are you doin' to that man!" hollered the butcher from down the boardwalk as he started toward the muggers.

"Quick, get his money pouch!" ordered Albert.

Eli grabbed at Talon's belt and snatched what appeared to be a money pouch and when his hand hit the butt of the Remington, he grabbed it as well. Without hesitating, the two fled down the dark alley behind the saloon and disappeared around the back of the building.

Chapter Three

Retribution

THE BUTCHER KNELT over the prone figure in the darkness and lightly slapped his face as he asked, "Are you all right? Hey, are you O.K.?"

A groan came from Talon as he raised his hand to stop the slap and he struggled thinking the man was attacking him but the butcher quickly assured him, "Whoa, I didn't do this, those other two did. Are you okay? Where'd they hitchu?"

"Ohhhhh . . .my head," he mumbled as he reached a hand to the back of his head, struggling to sit up. "I just stepped off the boardwalk and somethin' hit me . . . "

"Yeah, I saw that bearded bum draggin' you back here and I hollered at him. By the time I got here I saw the two of 'em duckin' round the corner yonder," he motioned toward the back of the building.

"You know who they were?" asked a groggy Talon as he struggled to his feet.

"I'm not sure, but I think they're a couple of laggards that've been hangin' around town lately. I've seen 'em in the Four Aces a time or two."

14

Talon, coming to his senses, reached to his belt and felt for his money pouch and knew it was gone, then his left hand felt the empty holster and he realized his pistol was also missing. He quickly felt for his Hawk and his knife and was somewhat reassured with their presence. He turned to the butcher and asked, "Would you recognize 'em if you saw 'em again?"

"Yeah, I think so, one of 'em's a pretty slouchy, somewhat fat man with a scruffy black beard and the other'ns pretty skinny, taller an' with a floppy, ragged black hat. I don't know their names, but I'm pretty sure they're the ones that did it."

"Oh, thanks for comin' when you did. They probly' woulda done more if you hadn't come along. I 'preciate it. Did you say you've seen 'em in the Four Aces?"

"Yeah, I usually stop off there for a drink 'fore I head home after work. I've seen 'em a couple of times."

"How 'bout comin' with me an' pointin' 'em out for me? I think I know who they are, I saw 'em earlier today sittin' on the boardwalk, but I wanna be sure."

"But you're just a young man and they looked pretty salty to me, you sure you wanna do this?" asked the butcher.

Talon let a chuckle escape and said, "Yeah, I'm sure. My Pa taught me to take care of problems when they happen and not put things off or let others handle 'em. So, I'll just take care of it my own self."

Talon bent down, picked up his hat and stepped up on the boardwalk to lead the way to the Four Aces saloon. Talon let the butcher push through the bat wing doors, giving him a chance to survey the crowd and the happenings of the saloon. He saw an unattended player piano banging away with the exposed roller grinding out an obnoxious song with the out of tune piano.

Several women were hustling drinks from the card players and idle drinkers at the tables and the bar. There was nothing unusual for any frontier saloon and the place was not overly crowded. The butcher took a place at the end of the long bar and motioned for the bartender to bring a beer as he nonchalantly looked over the crowd in the establishment. Giving a half-turn to look at Talon standing near the door, he nodded toward the far end of the bar. There the two men stood together with their backs slightly turned to the door as they both talked to one of the drink- hustling girls standing at the end of the bar.

Talon touched the brim of his hat, pulling it down slightly to obscure his face as he walked slowly to the end of the bar with a shuffling gait giving the impression he was looking for a card game to join. When he was behind the two muggers, he glanced over and saw his money pouch on the bar between them, there was no mistaking it as his for it had a beaded pattern that matched his belt as both were made by his grandmother, Laughing Waters.

With one step, he came between the two men, drew his Bowie knife and brought it down into the back of Albert's hand, pinning it firmly to the bar.

The skinny mugger screamed like a girl and grabbed at the knife with his free hand seeking to free it. Eli turned to face Talon and shouted, "What the . . . " to be met with the flat side of the tomahawk as Talon brought it against his head just above his left ear and dropped him like a scared coyote in a buffalo stampede. Albert continued to scream and everyone in the saloon stopped what they were doing and stood looking on in shocked silence. Talon replaced his tomahawk and reached to the bar for his money pouch. While Albert continued screaming and begging him to get the knife out, Talon calmly scooped up the loose change from the bar and dropped it into the pouch.

A big man in grey striped britches with a grey vest that boasted a five point star approached. Talon noted the buttons on his vest were about to pop as the threads holding them threatened to give-way under the strain of holding it together across the expanse of belly. Talon looked at the drooping grey whiskers of the man's mustache as the sheriff asked, "What's goin' on here? What's the idea of attackin' these men?"

"Attacking? I wasn't attacking, I was just takin' back what these two stole from me," replied Talon over the continuing moans and whines of Albert.

"Get this thing outta me!" screamed the skinny mugger. "You need to arrest that man, Sheriff, he attacked us!"

"Like I was sayin', you need to start explainin' yourself," instructed the sheriff.

Talon held out the money pouch and said, "These two men attacked me earlier tonight at the other end of town. The butcher there saw it, and they took this pouch and my pistol before the butcher got there and scared them off. I just came to get my belongings back."

"That there's my money, sheriff!" whined Albert, ". . .he took if right off the bar from in front of me. He can't do that!"

"How do I know who it belongs to?" the sheriff asked Talon.

Talon handed the pouch to the sheriff and said, "Look at the beading on the pouch, and look at the beading on my belt."

The sheriff noticed the matching beadwork and looked at the skinny mugger who had wrapped his hand with a dirty bar rag after the sheriff freed his hand. "How do you explain that?"

"Uh, uh, uh . . . that's just one o' them co. . . co . . .uh, you know, when things just happen to be alike, that's all," whined the skinny mugger. The bigger man, still on the floor began to stir awake and sat up holding his head. When he saw the sheriff, he looked to his partner, at Talon and back at the floor before struggling to his feet. The sheriff looked at him and at Talon and said, "Do you have anything else to say?"

"Ask that one about the pistol in his belt, that is mine too."

"What about it? Where'd you get that?" pointing at the pistol in Eli's belt.

"This?" he asked as he pointed to the pistol, "Why that's mine, I've had it a long time."

Talon said, "How 'bout asking him if he knows how to load it?"

"Load it?" asked the sheriff.

17

"Yeah, just see if he knows how to load it," said Talon assuming the big man knew little about the type of pistol he had in his waistband.

"How 'bout it? Show me how you load that pistol," ordered the sheriff.

"Well, just like any other'n, you stick the powder in and the lead, you know..." he said fumbling with the pistol trying to show the sheriff, but it was obvious he didn't know what to do.

Talon took the pistol from him and quickly dropped the forward lever releasing the cylinder and grabbing one of the spare cylinders from his belt he placed it in the pistol, locked the lever and handed it back to the sheriff. "And if there is any doubt, the serial number on that New Model Remington Army is AM19427, stamped on the left side of the barrel."

"All right you two, come with me," instructed the sheriff to the two muggers and turning to Talon, he instructed, "And you, young man, it would be best if you come to me instead of handling these things yourself."

"Yessir," answered Talon with a respectful tip of his hat as he replaced the pistol in its holster and tucked the money pouch into his belt. With a smile and a handshake to the butcher he turned to the bartender and said, "Give this man whatever he wants and here's the money to pay for it," as he placed some coin on the bar.

"Excuse me, young man," said an older gentleman as he approached Talon. He was dressed in a brown twill suit with a matching vest that held a gold chain strung across the front and disappeared into the watch pocket. The bulge in the pocket told of the large watch residing there. His outfit was topped with a small-brimmed, matching hat. Long sideburns of dark brown and a small moustache met a well-trimmed beard and told of his maturity, but smiling eyes told of his sincerity of character. He extended his hand for an introductory handshake as he continued, "My name is Ben Holladay, and I'm connected with the Overland Stage Company and you're . . . ?"

18

"I'm Talon Thompsett. Pleased to meet you, sir."

"And you as well. I wanted you to know I was very impressed with the way you handled yourself just now. As I see you up close, you don't appear to be too old, yet you braced those two men and didn't back down an inch. I like that in a man."

"Well, that's the way my folks taught me and I always try to handle my own problems."

"Yes, well, I'm always looking for good men and if you'd be interested and available, I'd like to have you come to work for our company. What would you say to that?"

"Well, as to being available, I just finished driving some cattle in to Camp Collins and I hadn't lined out anything to be doin' next, so I guess you could say I would be available. But as to interested, I would have to know more about what you are askin'," responded Talon.

"How about you stopping by the Stage station in the morning and we'll discuss it further, if that's all right?"

"I don't see why not. I'll be there right after breakfast, if that's suitable."

"That'll be fine, fine," said Holladay as he tipped his hat and left the saloon. Talon followed to return to the hotel. He'd had a full day and was anxious for a good night's rest. Tomorrow might begin a brand new chapter of his life and he wanted to be well- rested.

Chapter Four

Stage

BEN HOLLADAY LEANED back in his chair with his hands clasped across his stomach and said, "So, tell me about yourself, Talon, where do you hail from and such . . ."

Talon began with his beginnings on the ranch in the Medicine Bow valley and his wilderness education from the many extended family members and other friends. He also spoke of his parents' diligence at giving him and his brother the necessary education in the basics, including a solid grounding in the Scriptures. He concluded the brief summary with, ". . . and so I struck out on my own when I brought the small herd to Camp Collins."

"Impressive, impressive. And you've been acquainted with both the Arapaho and the Ute, that's a good thing. What do you know about the Cheyenne?"

"They're a good people, and are allied with the Southern Arapaho, but they're also a little more war-like than most."

"Hmmm . . . you're right about that. Well, what I'd like for you to do, to start, would be to ride shotgun on the stage that goes up the Overland trail to Fort Bridger and back. Of course, we won't expect you to make the full journey without breaks and relief, and there will be others that work the relay with you, but it can be a long journey. "

"Uh, I think you should know, my Ma and Pa were raised by the Arapaho. They're not Indian, they're white, but they were taken in by my Pa's Uncle and his wife, Laughing Waters, who is a Shaman with the Northern Arapaho and they were raised by them."

"Well, that's good, then you probably know a little about the Indian ways, am I right?" asked Holladay.

"Yes, and there's something else. When Ma and Pa started their ranch in the Medicine Bow valley, one of the men that worked with them married into the Ute people. His wife is a daughter of the chief of the Ute tribe up in that area and they're pretty good friends with them."

"Well, that's even better. The only thing that would be better than that would be for you to tell me you're on good terms with the Cheyenne," stated the older man.

"Well . . . their chief, Black Kettle, is the namesake of my Pa's grandfather, but I really don't know any of them. Pa tells me they had quite a battle with 'em shortly after they started the ranch but we haven't had any trouble with 'em as long as I can remember."

The big man sat up to his desk and chuckled as he rested his arms before him and said, "Young man, I think you and I are going to have quite a time with this stage line, that is, if you've decided to come to work for me."

"Yessir, I think I will. I've seen most of the country your coach's travel and that won't be new, but ridin' on top of the coaches will and meetin' all the folks will be interesting. So, sure, sign me on."

"Fine, fine, you're staying at Auntie Stone's place, are you not?"

"Yessir, I am."

"Then, let her know you'll be working for me and she'll keep any of your gear you don't want to keep with you and she always has a room for our men, so when you're back in town, you'll have a place to stay. As far as your horses, you can either leave them at the livery and we'll cover the cost, or you can bring them to the station and keep them with the horses here, your choice. The next stage leaves in about an hour, and if you're up to it, I'd like to have you aboard."

"Yessir, I'll be here."

Talon gave Smokey a boost up to the box and the dog scrambled on up to the top of the coach and after a cursory examination, flopped down just behind the seat with his snout resting on the rail facing forward. Talon stuck his Spencer and Henry in their scabbards in the front boot and using the front hub he stepped up to the box to situate himself. He strapped his Spencer to the rail along the top just behind his seat, put the Henry with the butt up by his leg in the front boot with his bullwhip coiled over the butt and sat back to await the driver. Within moments, the hostler finished with his adjusting of the harness and a grizzled, bow-legged whiskered man with a floppy grey hat pinned up at the front mumbled his way up to the seat and stopped suddenly as he looked at Talon and said, "Well, howdy Younker, whatchu doin' up hyar?"

"I'm your Shotgun, Charlie!"

"You don't say! Wal you don' look like you're old 'nuff to be outta yore diapers yet! Either yore mighty young, or I'm gittin' mighty old and don'tchu say nuthin' 'bout me bein' old or you won't get no older, neither!" threatened the old man and he grumbled his way into the driver's seat. After he quit wheezing and gasping he asked, "Who hired you anyway?"

"Mr. Holladay."

The driver whipped his head around so fast he almost lost his whiskers and he said, "Ol Holladay, hisself?!"

"Uh, well, I guess so, he said his name was Ben Holladay."

"Wal, I'll be hornswaggled, I didn't even know he was in the area. Ya don't say, wal, I guess if yore good 'nuff fer him, yore good 'nuff fer me." He took a longer look at the man beside him, sizing him up with his weapons and all, and said, "Can you handle all that hardware you're sportin'?"

"Yessir."

"Know anythin' 'bout injuns?"

"Yessir."

"What's that mean? Do ya, or don'tcha?"

"Been around 'em some, Arapaho, Ute, Cheyenne."

"Skeered?"

"Respectful."

"Hmmm, good answer, you'll do."

"By the way, my name's Talon. What would you like me to call you?"

"Wal, sonny, my name's Americus Josephus McGillicuddy. When I was a young'un, my Pa shortened it to Cus, and he would tell me, 'Do this Cus,' and 'Do that Cus,' but when my Ma would say 'Don't Cus' my Pa thot she was talkin' to him about his rather colorful language when she said 'Don't Cus' an' he would get cornfused, then I would get cornfused, an' Ma would just get mad, so to stop all the cussin' and cornfusin' it just got easier to call me Mac. So, that's the handle that was hung on me and that's purty much what I answer to now. Unless, of course, you call me Charlie or Jehu like lots of folks call us drivers."

"Alright, Mac it is," said Talon with a broad smile.

Mac leaned over and hollered toward the passengers, "Everybody sitcheated? We're 'bout ready to hit the road!"

With no retort but a few giggles, Mac righted himself and with both hands full of lines, he cast a wave with the lines and slapped the rumps of the team and they leaned into the traces and the coach lurched on its way. Starting off at a walk, Mac kicked the horses up to a trot as they pulled out of the settlement and started on the Overland trail to the North. Although the coach and Mac started their journey in Latham, there was a full day's travel ahead before rest would be had. A steady but easy climb from LaPorte to the station would cover about eleven miles before the station and barn would come into sight. Mac prided himself as a well-informed guide for the entire trip and enjoyed pointing out all the sites of interest to his new protégé. "Yeah, this is the new route. We used to go on that road a couple miles, west of hyar and our first stop was Boner, named after ol' Doc Boner. He's the sawbones that nursed that scalawag, Jack Slade, back to health after he was shot at Julesburg. 'Course it'd been better fer all concerned if he'd just let him die. Remind me to tell ya' 'bout him after we stop up yonder at Park Creek, He was a rascal that one, yessir, he was."

Mac's discourse trailed off as the coach pulled into the Park Creek Station for a quick change of horses and a short break for the passengers. As they pulled to a stop, Mac stepped down with a surprising agility and motioned for Talon to take a quick break and stretch his legs. He pointed behind the main building to the privies and started toward one himself. Talon looked back at the coach and noticed the door opening and a woman starting to exit. He stepped back to offer his assistance and to his surprise discovered all the passengers were women and most of them rather young. He offered them all his hand and they eagerly accepted his assistance and smiled their appreciation to which he tipped his hat and mumbled, "My pleasure, ma'am." When the coach was empty, he followed Mac to the privy and almost ran into him as he exited the small structure. Mac laughed and said, "I see you discovered the passengers," with his whiskers hiding his smile but his eyes revealing his mischief.

"Yeah, what are so many women doin' travelin' on a stagecoach, anyway? Where they all goin'?"

"Why, sonny, they's all mail-order brides," explained the old timer.

"What's a mail-order bride?"

"You go head an' do yore bizness, and I'll 'splain later."

Talon shook his head and disappeared into the privy. *This trip is gonna be interesting, I can tell already!* he thought.

Chapter Five

Explanations

"AND THEY'RE ALL GOIN' to California to those miners that sent for 'em, and they're gonna get married?" Talon asked incredulously.

"That's right," replied Mac as the two men rocked in rhythm to the constant movement of the stagecoach on the well-worn road. The six-up team was pulling well as they worked their way up and down the many grades through hilly country covered with juniper, cedar and pinion. It was dry country with scattered clusters of cholla and prickly pear cactus interspersed among the dark green of the dry land pinery. Piles of boulders seemed to be randomly stacked at the edges of hillocks that rose intermittently between deep, rutted ravines carved by flash floods making their way to lower elevations. The steady climb was evident by the changing landscape and the increased struggle of the team.

Talon shook his head in wonder at the revelation of what the women were doing. He had a hard time understanding the difficulty that anyone would have finding a husband or wife when there were already too many people in the world. And then to send half way across the country to someone you didn't even know and to agree to marry them was just more than he could comprehend. He shook his head again and said, "I just don't understand it, Mac, it just don't make sense to me. Oh, by the way, you said you were gonna tell me about that... what'd you call him, a scalawag?"

"Yeah, ol' Jack Slade. Well, ya see it's like this. Ol' Slade got into an disagreement of sorts with a fella named Jules Beni and ol' Jules shot him five times but Jack refused to die, an' that's when ol' Doc Boner brought him back 'round. Well, Jack went back to Julesburg, I think it was, found ol' Jules, tied him to a fence post, shot all his fingers off, one at a time. Then he shot him and cut his ears off! He kept them ears and showed 'em around and bragged on 'em too. He's the one what ol' Ben Holladay had start the station in Virginia Dale, but he ain't there no more. He went up into Montana, robbed a stage, got caught and they hung him. Yessir, he was a mess, that one was, yessir."

The trail took a slight turn and started down into a bit of a depression where Mac slowed the team down to a walk and said, "This hyar's Spring Gulch, over yonder a ways is where them 'rapaho used to spend their summers." With the horses continuing at a lazy gait, Mac pointed out a large promontory and said, "That yonder is what they call Signature rock. That's where a bunch a pilgrims think they's gotta carve their names in the sandstone. Guess they want sumbuddy to know they been here or sumpin'"

Mac pointed with his chin and asked, "Can you use that whip?"

"Yessir," replied Talon as he looked at Mac with a question on his face.

"Wal, we're 'bout to hit the Devil's Washboard an' it's a tough climb, if'n you can pop that thang o'er their heads an' make 'em lean into them traces a bit more, it might help us get to the top."

"Whenever you say," grinned Talon in response.

Mac continued to saw back and forth on the lines as they worked their way through the gulch and approached the steep, rocky incline. He slapped the horses with the lines and hollered "Heeeeyaaaaah!" and they lunged to get their start at the climb. Mac nodded to Talon and the young man uncoiled the braided black snake leather behind them and brought it forward with a resulting crack that sounded like a rifle shot as it echoed from the towering sandstone beside them.

The horses leaned further into their traces and dug their hooves into the rough trail beneath them and the coach rocked back on its thorough braces and then forward as the weight shifted to the front of the coach. Squeals came from the nine women as they were tossed about unexpectedly but there was no slowing down as the whip cracked again and Jehu shouted "Yeeeehaaaawwww" at the top of his lungs, as he slapped the lines on the backs of the team.

Twenty-four hooves clawed at the roadway and four wheels ground their way as the Devil's Washboard fought a losing battle to the determined corps of travelers. As they crested the top of the climb Mac leaned back in his seat and pulled the team to an easy walk to let them blow and recoup. He looked over at Talon and grinned, or at least made an attempt from under the grizzled whiskers, and said, "Yessireee, you'll do, you'll do!"

Mac slapped the lines to the team and once again they were off on the trail. He pointed to his right which was the northeast and said, "That over yonder is what they call Steamboat Rock. Does kinda look like one, don'tcha think?"

"I reckon, 'course I ain't never seen one, just some pictures is all. But I guess so," replied Talon.

The stop at Cherokee Station was another quick stop with just enough time to change teams and a short relief break for passengers and crew. Talon again assisted the ladies as they stepped down from the coach and was thanked by each one. A rather flirtatious one commented "Well, aren't you the gallant one? And way out here in the wilderness too, and good looking as well, my, my, my."

"Now Victoria, don't forget you're spoken for and besides, I think he's too young for you," chastised a more matronly woman. All the women were modestly attired in either homespun or gingham with nothing flamboyant or revealing, but the manner of some told of personalities that were less than demure. Talon was inexperienced in the ways of women of the world and his embarrassment was evident as he dipped his head and color flushed his neck and cheeks, but he refrained from any comment.

Mac hollered, "All right ladies, better get back aboard, this hyar ship's 'bout to leave the dock!"

With Talon's assistance, the women quickly re-boarded the coach, although some giggled as they stepped past him and he offered his hand. He was relieved to shut the door and climb back to his familiar seat with Mac. He focused his attention on Smokey and scratched the dog behind the ears, ignoring the driver. The old man just chuckled as he saw the young man's embarrassment, then he turned to his business as he slapped lines to the team and started on the trail again.

There was little change in the topography the twelve miles between Cherokee Station and Virginia Dale. Rolling hills with Juniper, Cedar, Pinion and the usual cactus and boulders provided little variety. The up and down of the trail was a continual workout for the team and driver alike but the Shotgun was always vigilant for any threat of danger. As they neared the flats of Virginia Dale they heard gunshots and Mac pulled the team up to listen. When the rattle of trace chains and the snorts and huffs of the horses stilled, they were certain that gunshots and lots of them were coming from the vicinity of the station. Smokey was on all fours and growling over Talon's shoulder as Talon looked at Mac. Mac returned the stare. "Whataya think, Mac? Should we go in? Or would we just be getting into trouble if we did?"

"I'm not sure young'un', but we can't stay here, there ain't no cover."

"Does the road drop down or is there any cover closer?" asked Talon.

"Well, now'd I think 'bout it, yeah. There's a dip in the road and some scrub oak and brush and a few trees there, an' it ain't too fer from the buildin's. We could prob'ly get that fer without gettin' seed, I reckon'"

"Let's go, but easy does it," directed Talon as he turned to get his Spencer from the scabbard.

As they approached the dip, Mac pulled the coach to a halt. The dip and trees did, indeed, obscure them from the battle and the combatants. Talon turned to Mac and said, "You stay here with the women, okay? I'll leave my Henry for you. I'm goin' closer and see what's goin' on and see if I can help. If I can, I will, but if not, I'll be back real soon."

As he dropped from the coach, he caught Smokey and the two started up the draw to make their way closer to the conflict. Within a short distance, the gunshots were louder and the war cries of the attackers more shrill. Talon bellied up the edge of the arroyo and with the shelter of a sage he surveyed the scene of the conflict.

It appeared to be a party of about eight Cheyenne trying to get to the horses in the corral between the barn and the station but the defenders were laying down enough of a cross fire that the attackers were unable to get to the corral. It was evident the attackers would not give up easily and would probably outlast the supply of ammunition from the defenders.

As far as Talon could tell, there was only one Indian down and none of the others appeared to be nursing any wounds. The attackers had gathered behind a cluster of Juniper and were starting a fire. Talon knew their next attack would be to fire the buildings and burn the defenders out.

Talon began to work his way closer to the location where the Cheyenne had tethered their ponies near their fire. As he located a couple of boulders with some scrub brush nearby, he mounted the boulders and took a firing position behind one and using another for a rest for his Spencer. He spoke to Smokey, "Smokey, get their horses!" and the dog took off on silent feet blending in the shadows. Talon waited.

As the sun dropped below the western horizon and dusk cast long shadows of darkness, he saw four of the attackers, with bows and long arrows heavily covered with pine sap, dip the arrows in the fire and start their approach to the station. The other four warriors held rifles and would provide cover-fire.

When the first shot sounded from the station, the warriors cut loose and the bowmen started forward. Talon fired and dropped the one closest to the building. The loud roar of his big Spencer betrayed his presence at the same moment Smokey's barking spooked the horses to break their tethers and flee. The Spencer roared again and another torch-carrying bowman fell, and then a third.

The fourth Indian had stopped in his tracks at the sight of the other three falling and his frozen stance was the last stance he would ever take before the leaden messenger of death sent him to his ancestors. The repeated roar of the Spencer and the rapid fire of the repeater caused the other attackers to think there were more riflemen and they turned to flee but finding their horses gone they milled around in momentary confusion. Another round from the Spencer, however, encouraged them to leave their fallen comrade when he fell at their feet, and they ran in pursuit of their horses.

Talon whistled for Smokey and when the dog returned with his tail wagging, the young man bent down and scratched behind his ears as he said, "Good boy, good boy, you done good, Smokey!" The two started their walk back to the stage staying out of sight of the station to avoid any mistaken shooting. When Mac saw him coming he waved his hat in the air and got a big grin from the old man.

"So, what was goin' on? Was it injuns?" he asked.

"Ah, just a couple of not-so-friendly Cheyenne wantin' to do a little campfire cookin', but I don't think those folks at the station were so inclined. But they're gone now, so we can go on in."

When the stage rolled in they were welcomed by the hostler and station keeper. Both stood with rifles at their sides and waved as the stage rolled to a stop.

"Howdy! Sounded like you folks was doin' a little target practice!" shouted Mac over the settling noise of the coach and team.

"You could say that, you know how it is, gotta stay in practice. Can't afford to get too rusty, what with all them injuns about nowadays," replied the station keeper. The hostler had jumped to his work of un-harnessing the team and taking them to the corral for water and feed.

"Looks like you got a new Shotgun ridin' with you," said Amos Gentry, the station keeper by way of asking a question.

"Yeah, this here youngster's, Talon, and that's his dog, Smokey. This is their first trip and I been kinda breakin' 'em in easy. You know how it is, don't wanna scare 'em off too soon," said Mac with a grin.

Amos turned to the passengers and said, "Folks, go head on an' stretch your legs, supper'll be ready in a bit. Ma's gonna have it on the table purty soon. There's a well an soap aroun' the corner if ya wanna wash up, an the privies are out back. You'll be spendin' the night here so make yourselves comfable."

Amos noted the big Spencer in the scabbard under Talon's arm as he made his way to the barn to find a comfortable sleeping spot with some soft hay. He watched as the young man surveyed the area as he walked between the buildings and knew this was the one that delivered them from the onslaught of the Cheyenne dog soldiers. He smiled and nodded his head and said in just barely more than a whisper, "He'll do, yessir, he'll do."

Chapter Six

West

A THIN SLICE OF MOON hung lonesome amidst the myriad of stars in the clear night sky with the belt of the Milky Way arching overhead like a bridal veil for some distant and unknown bride or perhaps, as a precursor for the many brides awaiting inside the Virginia Dale stage station.

Talon slipped out the back door and stood at the corner of the corral with one foot on the bottom rail as he allowed his vision to become accustomed to the darkness. He knew the dog soldiers would return for their dead and he wanted to ensure the only thing taken would be the bodies of their brothers. His Henry leaned against the corner post and his forearms rested on the top-rail as he slowly scanned the flats before him. He watched and waited with no desire for further death dealing but only for the protection of those within. He would allow the Cheyenne to gather their dead without any interference.

He heard the door open and close and the whisper of cloth against cloth and knew a woman or women were approaching. He whispered without turning, "Don't make a sound."

He was greeted by silence and stillness for a moment, then the movement came closer. There were two of them and they came one on either side of him. They looked at him, then in the direction of his gaze and whispered, "What are you looking for?"

"The Cheyenne will come for their dead. Just wanna be sure that's all they take."

"You mean you'll just let them come and not shoot them?" asked the one to his right with alarm in her voice and she spoke just above a whisper.

"Please, keep your voice down. If they know we're watching, they might want to take your scalp for a souvenir," he admonished with a whisper.

She unconsciously reached for her hair as if grabbing it would ensure its safety, then turned and hustled back into the station. Talon turned to the remaining woman and asked, "Aren't you going back in too?"

"No, I like the night, and I think I'm safe here with you."

He glanced back at the flats and turned for a better look at the woman beside him. She was one of the younger ones but not the flirtatious one. She was an attractive brunette with long ringlets to her shoulders over a gingham checked dress that had lace around the throat and a form- fitting bodice. She was a well-put-together woman and showed a certain confidence with fine facial features and bright eyes that showed a hint of mischief even in the darkness. Her smile displayed bright white teeth and full lips that parted as she said, "I *am* safe with you, aren't I?"

Talon stuttered a bit before he said, "Uh, yeah, I suppose."

"Well, Talon, my name is Susan, Susan Browning," she said as she extended her hand in introduction.

He tipped his hat and said, "Pleased to meet you, Susan, but it would probably be best if you went back inside where it is safer."

"Oh, but I would like to enjoy the night air for just a little bit longer, if that's alright," she said as she drew closer to Talon and put her hand on his arm.

Talon didn't know what to say or do so he just looked to the flats and searched for any movement, hoping to actually see an Indian that would save him from this woman. He was in luck as he watched a shadowy figure and another one run in a crouch to one of their fallen warrior's bodies. He motioned to Elizabeth with a finger to his lips and pointing in the distance toward the figures. She gasped and ducked her head below the rail as she whispered, "Oh dear!" and ran back to the door to re-enter the station. Talon continued to watch the Cheyenne while he let a long breath escape in relief thinking *I've never been so glad to see a dog soldier in all my life!*

The early start of the day had the sun on their right shoulder as the fresh team leaned into the traces and trace chains rattled their greetings to the morning dew that did its job of keeping the dust in its place on the rutted trail. Mac was in a cheerful mood as the matronly woman of the bridal troupe had been flirting with him all morning and he was feeling a few decades younger than he did when he'd turned in the night before. Talon thought sure he could see a smile through the tangle of whiskers that displayed the two tobacco trails alongside his chin. Jehu let the leaders have their head and set their own pace; with an early start, they were ahead of schedule and there was no reason to push the team this early in the day.

The terrain was unchanged with juniper, cedar and pinion up and down trail that followed the easiest course between the rolling hills and deep-cut ravines. There was still a slight upgrade but the pull was less than the days before and the team didn't seem to be struggling. A steady canter kept the coach in a smooth rocking rhythm that almost lulled Talon to sleep but every time he started to nod off, the crackly voice of Mac would shock him back to wide-eyed wakefulness to absorb some tidbit of information about the trail, the weather or the history of their surroundings.

Talon let his eyes wander to the west and he admired the eastern slope of the Medicine Bow Mountains knowing his home and family were just on the other side. The higher peaks were still crowned with snow but the late spring warmth was doing its best to rob the heights of its wealth of water and they would soon be scraping the blue with their bare granite peaks.

He knew his brother would be working the herd and looking for new calves and helping any new mother cows with their labor as need be, and would probably have the blonde-headed Elizabeth at his side. She had been their constant companion for the last decade, and Talon let out a long sigh as he thought of the times the three of them had shared. But he knew his brother Tyrell had won her heart and they would make a life together.

That was one of the reasons he was now on his own. A sudden jerk of the coach brought him back to the present as he grabbed the rail at the side of his seat. Smokey let slip a little whine at the unexpected bump but both dog and master soon realized there was nothing amiss.

"Didn't you say yore famly has a ranch somewheres abouts?" asked Mac.

"Yeah, sure did, if you look yonder at those snow-capped peaks, it's right on the other side there."

"Ya don't say, that's some purty wild country. Ain't that Ute country back in thar?"

"Some of it, that's also where the West Fork or the original Cherokee trail came through following the North Platte River in the bottom of the valley. That is 'fore this Overland Trail joined up with the East Fork and now most folks just follow it, which is fine with us, just keeps the pilgrims outta our country."

"Wal, don't you have trouble with the Utes?"

"Nah, they're plumb friendly. One of the fellas even married the chief's daughter, Spotted Owl, she's also a war leader and such."

Mac looked at Talon as if he'd grown another nose and said, "You spoofin' me?"

"No, I wouldn't do that."

"Boy, ever time I turn around you surprise me with sumpin' else, what's next?"

"Don't know, guess you'll just have to wait 'n see, now won'tchu?"

The coach crested the rise in the trail and the panorama before them was flat plains with scattered sage, cactus and small clusters of Indian paintbrush and blue lupine flowers. It was easy going for the coach and team with the trail straight and flat for several miles running.

Mac kept the team at an easy canter and continued his monologue of stage-line education for the new Shotgun. "The next station used to be called Dirty Woman on accounta the place was so dirty nobody wanted to stop there. Wouldn't nobody eat anything that woman ever fixed cuz there was so many flies ya' couldn't see what it were. She didn't never wash the pans and cups an' such so the compny just said- change teams an' keep ona' goin'. The Injuns took the place n' burnt it down, didn't kill her tho' n' didn't take her, neither. Everbody said even th' Injuns didn't want her cuz she only had one tooth. She finally ran off, nobody knows whar and nobody went lookin' neither. Folks what got it now do purty good. Now it's called Willow Springs cuz of the Willows and the Spring thar, as you can imagine. We'll be thar purty soon."

The flat land plains are deceiving with the low rise and fall of the land. Some of the slight dips can obscure a man on horseback and it was through one of those dips the coach dropped and came back up to the rise and spotted the small column of smoke among the distant willows. Mac said, "Somethin' ain't right, that's too much smoke."

"Are you sure? Don't look like a lot to me..."

"Nah, that's more'n 'nuff for any chimney smoke. Ya hear anything? Gunfire or anything?"

"No, nothing," replied Talon as he turned to look at Smokey for any sign of alarm but the dog still lazed behind his master.

Mac pulled back on the lines and walked the team to the willows to view the blackened remains of the stage station and barn. Portions of a corral still stood and corners of the log station still smoldered yielding the smoke. Mac pulled the stage to a stop and the nervous horses pranced amidst the smells of smoke and death. From the seat on the box the two men surveyed the scene and knew there was no living soul around. Talon pointed out the remains of two inside the station, another sprawled at what would be the barn door and another between the back of the station and the corral.

As Mac stepped down he said, "I'm gonna unhitch the team, water 'em and let 'em rest and eat a bit 'fore we head out. If you can find somethin' to bury 'em with, you can get started an' I'll help soon's I can."

Talon nodded soberly and turned to the door of the coach. He opened the door and told the ladies what to expect and said, "You can find some privacy back in the willows there, but don't go too far. Mac an' I will be buryin' these folks and then we'll be headin' on out." He stepped back and helped them down. He turned away and went to the remains of the barn to find a shovel to start his grisly task.

What would have normally been a few hours on the trail took the remainder of the day with several rest stops for a tired team. It was dusk when the coach pulled into the home station of Big Laramie. A quick crossing of the Laramie River was made easy with the corduroy of logs on both banks and the gravel bottom and the site of the large log structures promised a comfortable rest for the weary travelers.

Chapter Seven

Return

COMPARED TO THE accommodations and fare of the previous two days, the buffet before them was a feast fit for a king. A large platter of sliced roast beef adorned the center of the table and was surrounded by great quantities of potatoes, gravy, creamed asparagus and a mountain of, fresh from the oven, sourdough bread.

The ladies were a gaggle as they quickly seated themselves to partake of the sumptuous feast as if it would disappear before their eyes. Mrs. Newcomb and her helper, Mrs. Lyons, were well- experienced at feeding a crowd of travelers although they were not accustomed to all the travelers being gabby females. The large dining room accommodated the long table and allowed room for the men at the far end of the table. As Mac and Talon seated themselves, the station keeper, Captain Jack Newcomb wrangled a seat at the end of the table, dropping his crutches on the floor beside his chair and seating himself by extending his one stub of a leg with the other pulling his chair under the table. He had lost his left leg from the knee down during an early conflict in the war and returning home, assumed the job of station keeper at Big Laramie.

"So, Cap'n Jack, what's got these darn Cheyenne so riled up?" asked Mac as he reached for a slice of meat.

"Well Mac, from what I hear, we can blame it on a shave-tail lieutenant by the name of George Eayre. He's been leadin' a bunch o' them soldiers an' attackin' the Cheyenne camps in Kansas territory an' they ain't likin' it much," explained the station keeper.

"Cain't say's I blame 'em much, but that's a long way from hyar'bouts."

"Yeah, but when ol' Black Kettle of the Cheyenne and Niwot of the Arapaho signed that treaty at Fort Wise a few years back, they was a bunch o' them dog soldiers didn't agree with 'em and they been makin' trouble ever since. So, them soldiers that didn't get any fightin' in back East in the war, they been takin' it out on the Cheyenne and others. Trouble is, them soldiers with that shave-tail lieutenant have been hittin' the peaceful Indians instead of catchin' the Cheyenne dog soldiers that's doin' all the trouble makin'."

"Wal, I think it was them Cheyenne that hit us at Virginia Dale and we're purty sure it was them devil's that done in Willow Springs too."

"Yeah, probably the same bunch, they musta split up and hit both of 'em at the same time," surmised Captain Jack.

"We didn't see no bodies at Willow Springs, but there was a few at Virginia Dale, that's fer sure," explained Mac as he looked at his Shotgun. "What're we gonna do 'bout Willow Springs, I gotta take my coach back thru thar tomorry an' there ain't no team or hostler or nuthin' thar."

"I've already got men working on that. As you know, we're a home station here and I've got a couple of men that'll head out with you in the mornin' with two extra teams. They'll also have a wagon with some buildin' materials to work with for the station. You'll need to take it easy till you get to Willow Springs and then you can switch out and get on down the trail.

39

You'll get into Virginia Dale before too late, so you should be all right."

"Hummph, that's easy for you to say, but I reckon we'll make it- allus do," grumbled Mac around a mouth full of potatoes and gravy.

After their dinner, Mac and Talon walked to the other end of the L shaped building where the hay barn and stable would provide a soft place for their bedrolls for the night. Smokey trailed behind Talon and padded silently along. Mac idly commented, "Usually we'da went all the way to Fort Halleck, but what with the Injun uprisin' they shortened our route an' put on another coach. We'll switch off passengers an' swap mail pouches and head back to Latham tomorry if'n we can make it that fer without gittin' our hair lifted."

"Well, you're a cheerful cuss, Cus," chuckled Talon using Mac's original nickname taken from his given name of Americus.

"Heeheehee . . . ain't you the smart one," laughed Mac as he slapped Talon on the shoulder.

They found an empty stall full of fresh hay and rolled out their bedrolls and were soon fast asleep. Tired bodies rest well and without complaint when comfort is readily offered and gratefully accepted.

Talon noted the coach was much lighter for their return trip. The mail-order brides continued their journey with their considerable luggage in the company of the west-bound coach and the considerable load of mail pouches filled the boot and much of the foot space of the coach leaving the top of the coach to be loaded with the ladies' luggage. However, the east-bound coach that was captained by Mac and his Shotgun, Talon, had but two passengers; both men and a smaller assortment of mail pouches leaving ample room in the coach for the passengers. Smokey took his customary perch atop the coach just behind his master who was seated on the thin cushion in the box. Talon rocked easily to the now familiar sway of the concord. Keeping pace were the wagon and teams trailing behind and choking on the dust raised by the slow-going stage. It was an easy couple of hours until they pulled into the still smoldering site of the Willow Springs station and Mac leaned back against the lines and let loose with a long drawn out "Whooooaaaa there fellas, we're takin' a short break here an' we gotta swap out." He leaned over to tell the passengers, "Gennamen, we're gonna swap teams so you kin take a short break an' stretch yore legs, but don't go too fer or be too long!"

Talon stretched his leg to put his toe on the hub and dropped to the ground, looked up to catch Smokey as he jumped from the top and let him down to run around and sniff out the place. The hostlers were already unhitching the team and would soon have the next team ready, but Mac knew the new team would not be much fresher than the one he was leaving behind but it was only about fifteen miles on to Virginia Dale and they would have a noon break and a fresh team waiting.

As expected, Virginia Dale came into sight as the sun hit its zenith amidst a clear blue sky. As the coach pulled to a stop, the hostler quickly started un-harnessing the team and directed the Jehu to send his passengers inside for their meal. The two men from the coach quickly disembarked and stretched as they looked around.

One was short, bald and potbellied with a quick-talking squeaky voice who searched for the trail to the privy. The other man had a head of thick, grey-white hair and a massive moustache and thick eyebrows but a cheerful smile. His eggshell colored suit was rumpled but he tugged at the waistcoat to make himself somewhat presentable as he looked for a washbasin to freshen up.

He was noticeably pleased to find a basin on a shelf at the side of the building with fresh water, a bar of soap and a clean towel hanging from a nearby peg. He quickly washed his face, neck and hands and dried off as he said, "My, that is refreshing." He replaced the towel and noticed a stack of fresh towels at the end of the shelf and smiled broadly. He again

41

tugged at his waistcoat and straightened his jacket and walked to the front door of the station and entered to see what treats awaited.

Mrs. Gentry had laid out a fine meal for the few guests and the men were pleased with the offering of fresh baked sourdough bread, thin sliced elk meat, a mixture of potatoes, turnips, and greens that was very pleasant and all the men gave compliments to their hostess. The white-haired gentleman introduced himself and said, "Ma'am, my name is Samuel Clemens, and I've traveled over much of our fine land and many other places far and wide. I must say, you have set a fine table here in the middle of the wilderness that is rivaled by none I've seen in a very long time. Most recently I traveled from the West coast of America and the stations I had the unfortunate experience to visit quite recently were an abomination. Admittedly, I had come to expect more of the same, but madam, you have surprised me and quite pleasantly, I might add. I am very grateful for your kindness." He bowed before her, lightly grasped her hand, brought it to his lips, kissed it and smiled at her as she blushed in embarrassment.

As he turned to walk away, she brought her hand to her face and said, "My, my, I've never had anyone say such nice things before."

The others made their way from the station and Talon was the last to leave. He looked at Mrs. Gentry and said, "Ma'am, I never noticed before, but that man, he's Samuel Clemens, some folks know him as Mark Twain, he's quite well-known for the books he's written. I just thought you'd like to know, some folks say he's pretty famous."

She looked at the young man and glanced at the door as if she could see the white-haired gentleman and back at Talon with her eyebrows raised in a question. He nodded to her and walked out the door to join the others at the coach.

The fresh team leaned into the traces as Talon cracked the whip over their heads as Mac instructed. "I wanna see if'n we can make up some lost time. This part'a the trail's purty easy goin', so we can get to Cherokee in less'n hour, if'n we don't dawdle."

True to his word, just shy of an hour and with a lathered-up team, Mac pulled back on the lines and pushed on the brake lever to make the blocks squeal and lock up the back wheels and skidded the coach to a stop in front of Cherokee station. The passengers waited for the dust to settle and quickly stepped out to make the short jaunt to the privy and back to the coach in record time. The hostler was also quick with his work and Smokey barked his disapproval as the coach rocked back to start again on the trail.

Mac held the team to a canter in anticipation of the challenging Devil's Washboard. Although this direction would not be a pull, it would still be a challenge to make it down the steep grade, riding the brakes and trying to keep the coach from climbing up the horse's back legs. After the descent, Mac pulled the coach to a stop in front of the saloon at the bottom of the grade and hollered to the passengers, "Alright fellers, we got a quick drink break. One drink's all yore 'llowed, so make it quick!" Then, turning to Talon he said, "You gonna wetchur whistle, boy?"

"No sir, I ain't never developed a taste for the stuff, but you go 'head. Me'n Smokey'll stay here with the coach."

Mac quickly handed off the lines and jumped from the box as if he were ten years younger than his appearance portrayed. Talon took the time to survey the surroundings with a lingering look at the towering Signature Rock and the other sandstone features of the terrain. It was beautiful country, but also the kind of country that could easily hide a marauding party of Cheyenne. Talon unconsciously drew his Henry a bit closer to his side.

Just a few moments before the men returned, the grizzled features of Mac appeared over the edge of the box as he climbed back aboard his perch to resume his duties as Jehu.

They passed Signature Rock and were soon making dust on the trail through the scattered juniper and cedar. The rolling hills and ravines gave way to grassy plains that sloped away on both sides to the rising ridges that overshadowed the trail. The team was earning their oats as they pulled at a steady lope across the flats. In the distance, they could see the blacksmith shop that sat beside the trail near the "Horseshoe"- the natural amphitheater shaped grassy area that attracted many of the wagon trains as a natural camping spot. Their gaze shifted to the low area surrounded on three sides by the hills and saw the white bonnets of several wagons arrayed in a circular formation.

"Wal, they ain't in no hurry, what with it bein' so late already. They must be hangin' around an' havin' the smithy doin' some work fer 'em," said Mac as he motioned with his chin at the wagons.

Talon looked at the circular formation and said, "I don't think so, looks like some o' them got burnt. I think they've been hit by the Cheyenne."

Mac looked again as he sawed back on the lines and slowed the team, "You might be right. Mebbe we better go check on 'em, ya' reckon?"

"You're drivin'," said Talon.

Mac pulled hard on the lines to his right and the leaders moved off the trail in the direction of the wagons. As they approached, several men came out to meet them, each carrying a rifle, and one man, apparently the wagon master, said, "Man, are we glad to see you! Could you take some wounded back into town for us?"

"Maybe so, but what happened?"

"We were hit by some Indians at first light this morning. Caught us by surprise... we weren't expecting anything this close to a town an' all, but they sure hit us. As you can see, they burnt two wagons, torched a couple others we got put out. We had three people killed, two wounded and we think they carried off a couple girls and a boy."

For a moment, Mac and Talon were held speechless at the report, then Mac said, "Whatchu mean 'you think they carried off some'? Either they did or they didn't, which is it?" he barked angrily.

"Well, they're missing and one of the kids said he thought he saw them taken. So, yeah they took 'em," said the wagon master with his head hanging down.

"An' you ain't gone after 'em?" questioned Mac.

"Well, we don't know anything about the Indians, what they're gonna do or where they'll go, what could we do?"

"Pilgrims!" spat Mac. "Alright, git yore wounded in the coach, we'll get 'em to town and see if'n we can get the army to send somebody to help. Can't promise nothin' though."

Chapter Eight

Decision

IT WAS A SHORT HAUL to Park Creek and the hostler made short work of changing the team. Inside the coach, a wounded man was partially reclined and held steady by the drummer that nervously prattled on with a pretense of trying to console the wounded man when he was more scared and nervous himself. Mr. Clemens maintained his usual composure and kept the man from sliding around by nothing more than placing his foot beside his leg to steady him. On top, Talon had placed a blanket under the head of the prone figure of a woman and tried to keep her stable and comfortable with his hand on her shoulder. She was a middle-aged woman but it was evident from her attire and weathered features she had lived a hard life. Whenever she stirred to consciousness she rambled on about her babies and looked at Talon with imploring eyes and begged, "Please get my babies back, please!"

"Who are your babies, ma'am?"

"Oh, my Mary Sue, my sweet Mary Sue with her long red curls, and little Johnny with his curly red hair and freckles. Are you my little Johnny?" she asked as she looked at Talon with his dark red hair and sun-tanned face with barely obscured freckles. Her wounds and rising temperature were causing delirium. Her hands shook as she tried to touch Talon's face.

"Uh, no ma'am, but we'll get your young'uns back, I'm sure."

"Promise me, promise me!" she begged.

"We're gonna get the sojers from Camp Collins an' see if they'll go after 'em ma'am. I'm sure they'll bring 'em back."

"You, you get them. Promise me, promise me you'll bring my little Johnny and my Mary Sue back to me, promise me!" she insisted, once again reaching for his face. Her eyes were filled with tears and she winced with pain from the wounds to her chest. Talon noticed the blood spreading on her dress and knew the wound was opened and bleeding anew.

"Ma'am, you've got to try to be still, we'll be at the doctor's soon and he'll fix you up."

She squeezed his hand tightly and closed her eyes. Talon grasped her hand and looked closely to be rewarded by the swell of her chest which told of a breath taken and her continued life. It was a bumpy road and a fast trip. The horses were at a full gallop and Mac conducted the team as a maestro before a fine orchestra bringing music from the rhythm of the 24 hooves of the percussion section and the high octaves of the tinkling from the trace chains and the squeal of the leather thorough braces as the coach rocked its way to its destination. Both Talon and Mac were coughing and spitting as the dust curled up from the pounding hooves and sought to obscure their vision but the bouncing view of LaPorte soon rose from the sun-haloed dust cloud. Mac passed the stage station and pulled in front of the doctor's office and hollered at a bystander, "You there, help us with these folks! They need to get in thar to the doc!"

Several men stepped down from the boardwalk and stretched their arms up to take the woman from Talon and Mac. As soon as they moved away, Clemens and the stout drummer opened the door and handed off the wounded man to other men waiting to help. The crowd clamored with questions as to what had happened and when Mac gave his one word response, the alarm of "Indians!" was shouted almost in unison as everyone looked around as if expecting to see an attacking hoard descend upon them.

He then clarified, "No you idjits! It was up past the Park Creek Station and the Virginia Dale station and the Willow Creek station, but I wouldn't put it past them red devils to come down this fer, so ya' better arm yore selves!" He turned and grabbed the lines to take the coach back to the station and report and change teams. This coach was bound for Latham and there was still a long way to go before his trip was over.

They were greeted at the station with questions that were quickly answered with questions of their own. Talon interrupted Mac when he said, "I'm goin' to Camp Collins and see if I can get the Captain or somebody to take some troops out to find those kids that were taken."

"What kids?" asked the station keeper, Watts.

"There were two young women and a boy taken by the Indians and the woman we brought in is one of 'ems, Ma. She was pretty upset, of course, and we said we'd try to get somebody to go after 'em and see if they could get 'em back." Talon turned to Mac and continued, "Tell Mr. Holladay I'll be back as quick as I can."

"Holladay ain't here son, he's gone, and I'm in charge," said Watts. "And you ain't gonna get no soldiers to go after them folks cuz there ain't none."

"Ain't none... ain't none what?" asked Talon.

"There ain't no soldiers, at least not very many. I think there's only three or four of 'em left up thar to tend to things. Company B of the 1st Colorado, under Lt. Hawkins, was ordered off to Camp Sanborn. He said the 11th Ohio, I think it was, was gonna come in any day now but probly not till after the first of the month and they'd take over. But right now, ain't nobody up thar to help find anybody."

48

Talon looked at Mac and back at the station-keeper. Then he said, "What about the townspeople, ya think they'd be willin' to mount a posse or sumpin' to go find 'em?"

"If it's Injun trouble, they's more'n likely wantin' to stay right' chere and protect their ownselves and families. No, I don't think they'd be helpin' anybody but themselves, an' rightly so, we've seen 'nuff troubles of our own. But why didn't the wagon train folks go after 'em?"

Mac chimed in with, "Them pilgrims? They cain't hardly foller each other cross the prairie an' that's with them big white bonnets on them wagons in front of 'em, they couldn't find a track in a fresh snowfall cepin' somebuddy pointed at it, an then they'd ask a bunch o' fool questions!"

Talon looked at the ground and stomped his foot. Smokey looked up at his master and let a whine escape as if he was asking a question and Talon answered, "Yeah, I know boy, I know."

He looked at Mac and shook his head and asked, "You got anybody that can ride shotgun for you from here to Latham?"

Mac looked at the young man and at Watts with a question that was answered with an affirmative nod. Mac said, "You sure you wanna do this, son? Them Dog sojers is powerful mean and they is mighty riled up."

"If I don't, who will?" asked Talon.

"Nobody, I reckon."

"Pa always said, 'If it falls to you, don't shirk it, step up and get it done like a man,' and I can't let them kids go through what you and I both know they'd be facing. I practically promised their Ma that somebody'd go after 'em, so . . ."

Mac grabbed his hand and placed the other hand on his shoulder and said, "You know son, when I first saw you on top o' that box I had my doubts, but you shore proved me wrong. I reckon if anybody can do it, you can. Watch yore topknot!"

"I will, and thanks, Mac."

Talon snapped his fingers and man and dog trotted to the other end of town to the livery to gear up for the journey. A

49

quick stop at the general store provided supplies and additional ammunition and, as an afterthought, three more blankets, plates and cups. With everything secured on the pack horse, he started out by mid-afternoon to return to the site of the wagon camp. The Grulla was happy to be on the trail again and stepped out with long quick strides and covered ground like he was going to the mountains and his mustang stomping grounds.

The pack horse begrudgingly followed along and kept the lead line taut with his resistance but the occasional nip at his hocks by Smokey encouraged the laggard to quicken his pace. The long shadows of the surrounding mountains gave contrast to the many cookfires from the circle of wagons but they were a welcome sight for Talon. He was pleased when he was halted by a vigilant sentry and was directed to the wagon master's camp.

As he approached the wagon master's fire, Talon noticed the man standing had regained some of his self-importance and arrogance as he confronted the visitor to his fire. "And just who might you be?" he asked as he stood with one hand on his hip looking up at Talon.

Talon leaned forward, placed his forearm on his saddle horn and quietly replied, "We took your wounded folks into town. Both are at the doc's and bein' tended to but it'll be a while 'fore they can travel. The man'll be okay to move by tomorrow but the woman won't be for more'n a week or so. Thought you'd like to know."

"Oh, oh, yeah. Well, we can't wait that long. You say Mr. Tompkins could move tomorrow? So if we sent somebody after him, we could take outta here later tomorrow then. That'd be fine. But Mrs. Fredricks, well, she ain't got no family left n' no belongin's neither, since their wagon burned, she's better off just stayin' in town. We can't wait for her."

Talon looked at the ground and shook his head. He lifted his eyes to the man and asked, "Could I speak with the family of the other girl that was taken? I'd like to find out more about her, if I may."

"Well, what'dya wanna talk to them for?"

"I need to know about the girl and maybe get something the dog can get a scent from."

The wagon master said, "Just who are you anyway, comin' out here an' askin' all these questions?"

"I was the Shotgun on the stage that took your wounded in, my name's Talon Thompsett."

"Oh, oh yeah, now I remember you. Well, uh, my name's William Russell and I run this wagon train, but what do you wanna talk to the family for?" inquired the man who was obviously getting a little exasperated at the inquisitive young man.

"I'm going to see if I can get them back," he replied simply.

"You? Why you're just a young'un yourself!" laughed the big man, "an' I thought the soldiers from Camp Collins were gonna be comin'," stated Russell.

"They left, so there's nobody else, unless, of course, you would like to come along," offered Talon.

"Uh, uh, why no, I can't, we've got to get this train movin', We've got a long way to go," stuttered the man, "uh, the family's over yonder, they're the uh, the third wagon down that-away."

Talon looked in the direction of the man's pointing, back at the man who was now somewhat red-faced and said simply, "Thank you." He kneed his horse in the direction indicated and pulled alongside the family's cookfire. A woman knelt by a suspended pot and stirred the contents as she looked up at the mounted young man and said, "Yes, may I help you?"

Talon tipped his hat and asked, "Are you the family that lost a young woman to the Indian raid the other day?"

The woman choked back a sob and looked over her shoulder at her husband seated by the wagon with a rifle across his lap that he was in the process of cleaning. The man stood up and came to the fire and said, "You asked about our daughter?"

"Yessir. I understand your daughter was with the Fredrick's children when they were taken, is that right?"

"Yes, yes she was. Oh, step down and join us young man, my name is Fred LaForge and this is my wife, Eliza. Why are you asking about our daughter?"

Talon stepped down and extended his hand as he introduced himself and said, "I was the Shotgun on the stage that took Mrs. Fredricks into town and she spoke of her daughter, Mary Sue, and her son, Little Johnny."

Talon stood with the reins of his mount in his hand as the horses stood just out of the ring of light from the fire and Smokey dropped to his belly behind his master. "I tried to get some soldiers from Camp Collins to come look for the three, but they left a couple of days ago and there won't be any troops available for several weeks. When I was with Mrs. Fredricks, I promised somebody would go look for her youngsters and since there's nobody else to go, and I know the country and the Indians, I guess that means I'm the one that's goin'," he said.

Mrs. LaForge caught her breath as she put her hand to her mouth and muttered, "Oh, thank God!"

"Yes ma'am, I'm sure He's goin' to have to be in it all the way, cuz I sure can't do it without Him!"

Her eyes got real big as she looked up at him and she stood to her feet and stepped closer to him as she asked, "Do you know the Lord? Are you a Christian?"

"Yes ma'am, I am. My Ma and Pa made sure both my brother and I knew God's plan of salvation and that we accepted Christ as our Savior when we were younger." He laughed as he continued, "She said we were so ornery that we better get our hearts right with God before something terrible happened and we did."

Mrs. LaForge reached out and hugged Talon, catching him by surprise, but he stood stock-still and let her hug him and whisper, "Oh, thank God, thank God, He's answered our prayers!"

"Well, now, hold on just a minute. This is just the beginning. If you've been praying before, that's just practice, cuz you need to get serious about it now. I'll be goin' by my lonesome into some mighty wild country among some blood-thirsty Cheyenne dog soldiers and I've gotta find these young'uns mighty soon, so it's gonna take a lotta powerful prayin' on your part to make that happen."

"Oh we will, we will. But right now, you need to sit down and have some supper. You're not goin' off in the dark are you?"

"No ma'am, I'll get an early start in the morning."

"Fine, now you take care of your horses and we'll have supper together and you stay with us now, y'hear?"

"Yes'm."

Chapter Nine

Hunt

A THIN LINE OF GREY marked the silhouette of the eastern horizon with a slightly deviated straight line. The flats before him were deceptive and a newcomer would think there was no variety to the terrain. But Talon knew the country before him was wild and forbidding with challenges too numerous to name but ample to claim the unwary.

He knew the flats that lay immediately to his east were well-watered plains with buffalo grass and wildflowers that attracted deer, antelope and buffalo. The mesas and plateaus beyond cradled deep gorges, ravines and canyons between them and sheltered considerable growth of juniper, cedar and pinion with more varieties of cactus and dangerous varmints than he cared to consider. He always marveled at the variety of colors of the clay and adobe that clung to the hillsides and the sandstone castles that were carved by the runoff from the desert rains.

He remembered the times he and his brother discovered petroglyphs and pictographs inscribed by the ancients that told of hunts of animals now extinct and peoples long forgotten. It was a marvelous land but it also held numerous places where war parties could easily be hidden.

He wished he had his father and grandfather to counsel with or perhaps his grandmother, Laughing Waters of the Arapaho and Spotted Owl of the Utes, to give him guidance as he sought to find the renegade Dog soldiers that had rebelled against the leadership of their own people. But this was a quest of his own and there was no one to turn to for guidance or advice. He would have to tap deep into his own memory and teachings if he was to be successful in this rescue.

The first rays of the rising sun bent across the horizon and searched their way across the sky to light the way of the wanderer. With the brightness in his face, Talon bent his head down to allow the brim of his brown felt hat to shield his eyes as he guided his mount with knee pressure.

The trail of the attackers was easy to follow, ten or twelve mounted horses running had turned up the soil considerably, but he knew they would soon slow and maybe even divide their number, making his task more difficult. But for now, he continued. The flats gave way to the rise of the hillside to his right with scattered trees and cactus dotting the slopes between the boulders.

The slope rose to rim-rock that appeared as a fence line of standing granite to mark the flat top of the broad plateau. To his left, the flat dropped away to a red and tan clay streaked hillside ribbed with gullies carved by spring rain runoff. The trail of the Cheyenne was slightly dimmed by the winds that often whipped through the valleys and ravines, but the many horses made ample sign. Talon noted a protruding shoulder of sandstone that marked a ravine that appeared to have some source of water and he reined his mount into the cut.

A small cluster of stunted willow betrayed a spring and a pool of water with grass-lined banks inviting him for a mid-day break. Stepping down, he loosened the cinch on the Grulla and the cinch on the pack for the bay pack-horse, but left them tethered together and allowed them to drink their fill and graze on the grass. He grabbed a handful of jerky, took a seat against the sandstone cliff just back from the spring, and surveyed the valley below.

The Cheyenne had a full day's start on him, but traveling in a group and with captives, they might not move as fast as usual. He knew they would keep a look-out on their back trail to see if anyone followed, but since there had been no pursuit for the entire day following the early morning attack, he was pretty sure their vigilance might be somewhat relaxed. Also, they would probably be pre-occupied with their prisoners, but he didn't really want to dwell on that as there was no telling what a bunch of renegades that prided themselves on their warrior ways would do with the captives.

All the attacks had been along the Overland trail and had focused on the stage stations and the wagon train, probably to get horses and weapons. They were successful getting horses at Willow Springs, but had failed at Virginia Dale. That's probably why they tried the Wagon Train, but all they got from the train were the captives, and for what purpose? The captives wouldn't be good for anything and would only slow them down on raids and such. They might be able to trade them off though, but where and to whom?

No place that he could think of and he knew that what they really wanted was rifles, ammunition and horses. That meant they would probably just get rid of the captives or . . . what? Talon was stymied, but he knew he had to keep going and find them as soon as possible- no matter what.

This was rugged country. He and his Pa and brother had only been through this area once before and that was on a trip to the small town of Cheyenne, only to find there wasn't much to the town and their trading trip had proven unfruitful but informative. This terrain made it difficult to make a surreptitious approach as the vegetation was sparse and scattered but his singular advantage lay in the color of his mount and his attire that blended well with the dry terrain of sandstone and adobe. The pack horse was a dark bay color, but the dusty countryside soon coated him with a fine dust that blended well with his surroundings.

The flat-bottomed shallow canyon he now traveled was a dry streambed of gravel and sand that saw moisture only when the rains were sufficient to overwhelm the capacity of the nearby hillsides and wash down the ravines to fill the thirsty bed. The nonappearance of any greenery told of a long-time absence of moisture and the horses shuffled through the loose sand along the winding course. The click of the Grulla's hoof on a stone echoed off the canyon wall and startled Talon so he reined up the horses and listened. He stepped down with his Spencer in hand, ground hitched the Grulla, and worked his way up the dry adobe of the shoulder to his right. He slowly lifted his now hatless head over the crest to look down the course of the long canyon before him. There was no evidence of life, but something still bothered him and he remained motionless and watched and waited. The horses took advantage of the break and stood hipshot with eyes closed while they waited. Smokey lay beside his master with his nose next to Talon's elbow and watched.

There! Talon moved only his eyes and watched. The slow movement of a man backing away from a large boulder and past a small patch of scrub brush. He moved slowly down the hill just below the ridge of the ravine with only the top of his head showing and disappeared. Talon waited and listened. Then the click of a hoof on a stone, and nothing else. Still, Talon waited and Smokey stayed motionless knowing what his master watched. After a full quarter of an hour, Talon backed away from the ridge and walked back down to his mount. He stepped into the stirrup, swung aboard and started again on the gravel and sand streambed to quietly continue down the bottom of the wide arroyo.

When he neared the place where he saw the warrior, he checked the tracks and knew this man was a rear guard and was returning to his people to give his report. Talon was certain he had not been seen but he also knew they were being extra careful of their back trail and he would have to be cautious as well.

Within another hour, the arroyo played out as the stream bed dropped off the edge of what would have been a waterfall in wetter times. He noticed that the trail, now fainter from the wind in the canyon, turned to follow a shoulder along the edge of a large escarpment that surrounded a broad plateau. Dusk was fast approaching and he searched for a good place to make a camp that would provide sufficient cover and graze for his animals.

He no sooner thought of it than a bend of the trail offered a deep ravine that cut into the shoulder of the hillside and behind a thick cluster of juniper lay a small patch of buffalo grass and a good flat area for his camp. A smoke blackened circle of stone showed this site had been used before and probably repeatedly by others that traveled this trail, but it would serve his purpose well.

He disdained the idea of a fire and made a cold camp after giving his animals drinks from his water bag by using his cook pan. Talon wiped them down with a handful of buffalo grass and they drank deeply and appreciatively before rolling in the dust nearby. Although he would like some coffee, Talon chose to just enjoy his jerky and water, sharing both with Smokey, and turned in for the night. He knew his horses and Smokey would be on watch through the night and he could sleep well without worry.

Chapter Ten

Sighting

A GENTLE TOUCH FROM smokey brought Talon instantly awake. The dog often awakened his master with the simple nudge to his arm with a soft paw that wasn't alarming but still accomplished the desired effect of alerting his master of danger. Talon peered from slit eyes as his fingers gripped the hilt of his Bowie knife and the butt of his Remington .44.

Moving slowly, he turned his head to survey his camp and seeing nothing nearby he rolled from his blanket to take position in the shadow of the nearby sandstone cliff. Smokey crawled beneath the low hanging branch of the nearby juniper and waited. The soft sound of moccasins came as a shadow moved closer to the blankets bunched below the saddle. The sliver of moon provide just enough light for Talon to make out the crouched figure of the Cheyenne with raised tomahawk but Talon looked for more. As the warrior neared what he thought was the sleeping figure of the white man, he stepped forward and brought the hawk down in what would have been a death blow but before he realized his mistake the Remington blossomed orange from the shadow and dealt death to the attacker.

Suddenly a blow knocked the pistol from Talon's hand as a tomahawk from an unseen attacker struck the barrel of the weapon and ricocheted to Talon's wrist. Talon. He gasped in surprise but reacted quickly and plunged his razor-sharp Bowie knife up into the side of the warrior simultaneously with Smokey sinking his teeth into the hamstring of the Cheyenne.

The Dog soldier screamed in shock as Talon yanked his blade free from his ribs and drove it in again burying it to the hilt and twisting the long blade as the warrior squirmed his death dance and dropped to his face at Talon's feet with blood forming a pool of blackness in the moonlight. Talon stepped back and scanned the darkness for any other threats but saw none.

Smokey padded around the perimeter of the camp searching for any sign of danger and returned to Talon's side for his "Atta, Boy" and Talon dropped to one knee and scratched his friend behind his ears, whispering his approval.

They sat quietly together and listened before Talon moved the bodies of the attackers away. When he returned, the grey light began to chase the darkness from the black canopy and the young man decided to take the time for coffee, bacon and warmed-over biscuits. The dry wood gave little smoke that was filtered by the overhanging juniper and the morning light dimmed any possibility of the light of the fire betraying their presence. But he knew the drifting odor of both the bacon and coffee would be easily detected so he made quick work of the breakfast and was soon ready for the trail.

He swung a leg over the saddle but before he started out, he sat for a moment in thought. He looked up at the rising plateau above him with the escarpment of granite that held the flat-top as a sentinel of the surrounding plains and considered. The Cheyenne knew he was following and when their two scouts failed to return, they would be expecting him to be hard on their trail and would lie in wait putting him at their mercy.

If he could only know where they were beforehand, but how? Of course, the plateau! He spurred his horse out of the ravine but instead of taking the trail in pursuit of the Cheyenne, he turned back on the trail in search of another route that would take him around the big butte. Living in this country, he knew the mesas, buttes and plateaus, all names of different sized flat-tops, were of a basically round shape and appeared as islands in the plains. If he could find a trail to the top from the back side of the butte, he would have a promontory with a view of the entire area and would likely be able to spot the Cheyenne without them knowing.

He gigged his horse to a trot and searched the ground before him for any sign of an off-shoot game trail that would lead around the butte. He had traveled less than two hundred yards before he spotted what might be a path that cut through a cluster of cholla and pinion to make its way around the shoulder of the big butte. He slowed his pace as he searched the hillside and escarpment for any sign of a break in the granite talus.

As he lifted his eyes to the top of the rim-rock, a long shadow caught his attention. He reined up and examined the slope leading up to the apparent break in the towering wall. A faint trail seemed to lead across the rubble and disappear into the break. He followed the grey line back and down as it dropped behind a thicket of juniper above the trail.

Talon dismounted, ground-tied his mount and with Henry in hand, walked to the trees to find the beginning of what he thought might be the answer to his search. He kicked out a big eared jackrabbit from under a weather worn cedar and stepped over a clump of prickly pear but soon found the beginnings of the trail. There was little sign of use, no recent tracks of anything but a desert Muley, perhaps a week past. He stood on the path and looked up the length and could see where it disappeared into the cleft. Looking again at the tracks of the mule deer, he saw only those tracks going up the trail and none coming down. *Well, he either sprouted wings, or there is definitely a way to the top through that break in the rocks, so maybe that's my answer,* thought Talon.

He returned to the horses, sheathed his Henry and decided to lead the horses up the track. Walking before them, he noted the sharp shreds of granite alongside the trail while on the path the accumulation of wind-blown and well-trodden dirt gave a smoothness to the trail. It was narrow and the drop off to the jagged stone was shear and intimidating but the horses were confident as they followed Talon up the steep route.

Nearer the escarpment, the path became more rock-strewn and difficult, he stepped carefully and he let the horses pick their way slowly. Suddenly, the pack horse nickered and fell to his knees. Talon looked back and saw the animal trembling and with wide eyes that begged for help, refusing to move. Talon dropped the lead on Dusty and carefully side-stepped beside his horse with his arms outstretched for balance and made his way back to the still-trembling bay. The pack horse moved his head slightly to look at the path and the drop off and back to Talon as the young man spoke softly to him. Talon reached down and took hold of the lead rope. Gripping it with his right hand, he reached out and stroked the cheek of the bay to calm the animal. He stood close to the horse's head which was at the level of his knees, and pulled on the lead rope, as he spoke, "All right boy, up we go, come on now, you can do it."

Encouraged, the horse stretched out one leg and struggled to stand, and lifted himself up using the stabilizing lead rope for help and stood, still trembling, as Talon continued to stroke his cheek and neck to calm the animal. Talon draped the lead rope over the neck of the pack horse, sidled along Dusty and picked up the reins of his mount and started back up the trail. After a few steps, he looked back at the pack horse and saw he was timidly following, but following nevertheless, and they continued with Smokey leading the way.

The dog disappeared into the dark shadow of the break in the escarpment but his muted yip told Talon that Smokey was on the trail. As he entered the narrow cleft, he saw the trail take a switch back around a jagged chunk of granite and then make a straight up ascent to the top. It would be easy access for a mule deer or other creature of the plains, but it would be a challenge for the horses. He stopped and let the horses rest in the shadows while he moved ahead to check out the slope. He started up the steep portion, noting it would have reasonably good footing with little loose shale, but it was steep for about fifteen feet before cresting at the top. But as he looked back at the trail, he realized they were committed anyway because there was no place for the horses to turn around without stepping off or falling off the steep slope. The only way out was up.

Talon removed the bridle from Dusty and replaced it with a sturdy halter and a strong lead rope. He led the horse to the foot of the steep portion of the ascent and stopped him. Talon moved up the gradient the length of the lead rope, turned and dug in his heels and spoke to Dusty, "All right boy, just a little ways now, come on." Talon pulled on the lead and encouraged the horse to start the climb and as the horse started to dig in his hooves, Talon backed up the slope to the crest. As the horse humped and dug in for traction the man pulled on the lead to give the horse additional leverage and pulling and pushing together the horse made the climb and humped over the crest to the top and stood spread legged and breathing heavily as Talon stroked his neck and spoke to him.

With deep breaths, Talon returned to the waiting pack horse that had fearfully made his way to the bottom of the ascent. Talon removed the packs and panniers and set them aside. It would be too difficult for the bay to make the climb with the heavy burden and not worth the risk. Talon latched onto the lead rope and repeated the climbing action to successfully bring the pack horse to the side of Dusty. Taking a coil of rope from his saddle, he went to the packs and panniers, secured them in a bundle and climbed back up the gradient to secure the rope to his saddle and pull the parcels to the top.

 He re-rigged the pack horse and taking a few moments for man and beast to rest, with each having a share of water from the water bags, they soon set out for the edge of the plateau that would provide a vista of the plains below and hopefully, a view of the Cheyenne.

Chapter Eleven

Captives

TWO BEARS WAS THE son of the Cheyenne war chief, White Antelope, and was chosen to lead the Dog soldiers three summers past. His friend, Broken Nose, had been with him since childhood and stood beside him as they talked about the captives now seated against the sandstone cliff in the afternoon shade.

"They are nothing but trouble, you should not have taken them," stated Broken Nose again. They had argued before but nothing had been resolved. Two Bears was well known for his stubborn nature but he had proven himself an effective leader of the Dog soldiers.

"We have not taken captives before and this will show the whites they are weak before us!" proclaimed Little Antelope as he walked up to the two leaders. He continued, "The blue coats have killed our women and children and we should do the same to these. It is a waste of time and food to keep them alive," he spat the words with hatred.

"We are not the blue coats and we are not like the whites. These are worth trading for guns or horses, the whites are weak and will give much to have them back," declared Two Bears.

"But where can we trade them?" asked Broken Nose.

"Maybe at a stage station or ranch, we send the boy to tell them we have the women and will trade," suggested Two Bears.

"What about the one who follows?" asked Little Antelope, "Raven and Red Hawk have not returned."

"You will take Running Wolf and go find them. Then we will see to the one who follows."

Ginny leaned against Mary Sue and whispered, "They're talking about us, Mary Sue, what do you think they're gonna do?"

"I don't know, Ginny, but I wish they'd loosen these rawhides they got us tied with, they're rubbin' my wrists raw, and I'm loosin' feelin' in my hands. How 'bout you, can you feel your fingers?"

"A little, I think mine are looser'n yours, but they're still tight. At least we're in the shade here. Ya think they're gonna feed us anything?" asked Ginny.

"I dunno, and I'm not too sure I'd wanna eat anything they'd feed us anyway. But I sure am hungry, aren't you?"

"Yeah," then turning to the boy she asked, "How you doin' Johnny, you alright?"

"I been better, that's for sure, but I guess I'm okay," he answered.

All three captives were bound hand and foot with rawhide strips and had been tossed against the sandstone cliff with little concern for their comfort except the shade provided by the overhanging cliff. The thicket of Juniper on the slight sloping hillside provided both cover and a view of the shallow valley and dry stream bed below. Dropping away from the sandstone ridge behind them and fading away before them was a long line of red and tan clay ridges and ravines aligned like marching soldiers parading to the western horizon. Below the clay ravines a green- bottomed valley told of a small stream that carved its way through the dry, rugged countryside. Rising opposite the clay ravines was a long rim-rock lined ridge that marked the western boundary of sight before them. The facing slope of the distant ridge was pock marked with boulders and the dark green of cedar and pinion promising little but more desolation.

The girls had fallen silent as they pondered their predicament and Ginny spoke from despair as she said, "Even if we could get away, where could we go and how?" as she looked at the desolate land before them.

"But we can't just give up, Ginny, we don't know what they'll do to us or Johnny either," pleaded Mary Sue. "I think they killed my Pa and maybe Ma too. I saw 'em both fall before that big Indian over there grabbed me," she said as she motioned toward Two Bears with her chin. "And I think that skinny one wants to kill us or somethin', the way he looks at us and such," she said as she looked at Little Antelope.

"Well, we've been lucky so far, but if they make us walk another step I think I'll just lay down and die! I've got blisters on my blisters and my feet hurt so much, I just can't walk no more," declared Ginny.

They watched the group of three warriors talking near the tethered horses as they occasionally looked in their direction. They didn't notice as one of the other men slowly approached from behind a twisted cedar just below the patch of cholla and prickly pear at the edge of the juniper thicket. He was on them without warning, and grabbing Ginny by her hair he twisted her to the ground and grabbed at the sleeves of her dress, tearing them as he cackled in glee.

The girls' screaming had caught the attention of the other men and they came running. The attacker grinned maliciously as he pulled at the tight-fitting bodice seeking to tear it from Ginny's body but he was knocked away by a kick from Two Bears. As he fell, he kept his grip on the one sleeve of her dress and tore it from her arm, ripping the side of her dress and exposing a generous amount of flesh. Two Bears followed the rolling figure of Running Wolf repeatedly kicking him and shouting his disgust and anger. Although his words were not understood by the women, the intent was clear and they realized the leader of the raiders was also their protector.

Ginny struggled to right herself and scooted next to Mary Sue, sobbing as she watched the two men argue over the conflict. Running Wolf got to his feet and with a scowl he muttered his assent to whatever demand was made by Two Bears and walked away, joined by Little Antelope for their assigned tasks.

As Two Bears walked by the women he looked at them but his expression revealed neither pity nor compassion and bordered on disgust. He spat on the ground and looked to the rest of the men gathered by the small cookfire. Taking his place at the circle, he began talking with them, obviously about the captives.

"Now what are they going to do?" asked Ginny.

"I don't know, but at least that one is gone. I wish somebody would come for us, but there's nobody who would, is there?" said Mary Sue.

"If we could get a knife or something to cut this rawhide, maybe we could get outta here," suggested Johnny.

"And then what, Johnny?" asked his sister.

"I don't know, but anything's better'n just waitin' fer 'em to kill us," he suggested.

"Well then, let's watch and see what we can find, or try to get free. Maybe we could do it after dark and get a horse or something," said Ginny. "I'm willing to try, aren't you?" she asked, looking at Mary Sue.

"Like Johnny says, I guess it's better than waiting for nothing."

"We will go to the east where there are some white man ranches. We will see if we can trade the women for guns or horses. If we cannot, then we will do away with them. We will keep them for two more days, no more," stated Two Bears to his men.

The warriors looked at one another and nodded in agreement with some grunting their approval as they looked at the women. The one called Lone Eagle asked, "We can use them until then?"

"No, but if we cannot trade them, you can do what you want."

Again, there were nods of agreement from the circle of warriors. Lone Eagle stood and looked at the women, turned to the others and declared, "The one with flaming hair is mine." The others busied themselves with preparing something to eat but they neglected the captives as they gorged themselves on the half-cooked meat of a recently killed antelope.

Chapter Twelve

Located

THE PLATEAU WAS EASILY a mile across and like most of the flat tops was almost barren. Patches of buffalo grass and scattered clumps of prickly pear did little to break the monotony of the flat. There was one small cluster of scraggly juniper on the Northwestern edge near where Talon sought a promontory outlook. He tethered his horses in the scant shade, retrieved his spyglass telescope, a Broadhurst Clarkson model traded from an old Scottish sailor, and went to the edge of the granite escarpment.

He bellied down and surveyed the area below before using the scope. He watched for movement and unconsciously rubbed the ears of Smokey as he lay beside him. He looked in the distance at the many colors of the clay walled ravines, the scattered trees and strewn boulders. From this perspective, he imagined God standing on high and scattering the different soils and seeds like a farmer walking through his field. With handfuls of stones like gravel in the hands of a man, the creator would sprinkle the earth with boulders and piles of rock as decoration for his vast garden. It was indeed an amazing and diverse world, but this wonder of creation now held creatures that kept others captive and it was his task to return them to freedom and hopefully unharmed.

He looked for areas that would provide cover and vantage points for the raiders, for these were no pilgrims or newcomers to this land. They knew this country even better than he and that meant he must be at his best if he expected to accomplish the rescue. But he was born competitive and his entire life was one of competition with his twin brother and those around him.

Talon knew what it was to rise to the task and to match wits with others. He remembered the times he and Tyrell had bested the youths of the Ute village in contests of hunting and fighting. Their skills had also been tested by the men on the ranch and Reuben, the former waterfront stevedore, had challenged them time and again in ways never before seen but they prevailed. Even their own father, Caleb, who had his skills honed by the men of the Arapaho and Crow, had schooled them in the skills of the wilderness and helped them to understand the ways of other Indians and white men as well. But now, he was alone, and three lives depended on him. The lives of two women and a boy that didn't even know he was near or that he would try to free them. He wondered if they had given up hope or if they still struggled and prayed for deliverance.

Still he scanned the area below, carefully watching and using his peripheral vision for any indication of movement. He had been taught that he could see more without looking directly at the object and he slowly moved his eyes to and fro across the landscape, searching and hoping. A big mule deer buck kicked a couple of doe out of the trees before him and followed them down the clay hillside to the stream below. A scream from a circling golden eagle diverted his attention to the cloudless blue sky overhead as he watched the majestic king of the sky search the same countryside for his dinner. The eagle suddenly folded his wings and changed his direction to return to his nest high on the distant cliff of the granite escarpment. *Something moved below he didn't like, what was it?* mused Talon as he returned to scanning the landscape before him.

Then he saw two mounted Cheyenne coming at a canter from his left and the direction of his morning's camp. *I bet they either found the horses or the bodies of those two that jumped me this mornin' an' now they're here to tell the tale. Good, now I'll know where the rest of 'em are.*

To his surprise, they reined in to a thick cluster of Juniper almost directly below his promontory. He crawled closer to the edge and looked over the edge of the sheer cliff. The granite fell away in a steep drop almost a hundred feet, a slight slope to a shelf of sandstone and then nothing. As was often seen, a seam of sandstone formed a shelf that held the scree or rubble and formed a cutback below. This cutback was the overhang that shielded the captives from Talon's view and the thick Juniper prevented him from seeing the camp of the Cheyenne. When the two returning warriors caught his attention, they had also revealed the location of the camp.

His scope wasn't necessary even though he was well over two-hundred-feet above them, their animated conversation told him the two returnees had indeed found evidence of the kill. He watched as they motioned back in the direction of the camp, but it appeared they also told of his tracks leading away. He unfolded his spyglass and watched. The facial expressions on the men gave Talon the impression the warriors were upset at the deaths of their men, but gloating that the white man had turned tail and left. The big man, apparently a leader, walked toward the overhang grinning and gesturing. *That must be where the captives are,* thought Talon.

Ginny pushed against the shoulder of Mary Sue and whispered, "Here comes the big man, he's happy about something." The girls watched as Two Bears approached with Broken Nose a few steps behind. The two men stopped within a couple of paces of the girls, looked down at the bound captives and grinned. Two Bears laughed and said in broken English, "White man come for you but our warriors chase him away. He leave like scared rabbit."

"You speak English!" exclaimed Mary Sue, "Can you give us something to eat?"

"You no eat. We trade you for guns, or we kill you," proclaimed Two Bears somberly and turned away to return to the campsite.

"Who do you think it was that came for us?" asked Ginny.

"I don't know of anybody that would. Maybe he's lying just to provoke us or something."

"But he said they will trade us... who to?" inquired a very scared Ginny.

"I don't know, maybe a rancher or trader or . . . I don't know, but anybody'd be better him! He said he'd kill us," reminded Mary Sue. "We've got to try to get free, somehow."

"I think I might be able to get my hands loose if I keep workin' at it," said Johnny.

"Let's all keep at it, we've got to keep trying."

The voices from below carried to Talon but most of it was unintelligible. He did, however, hear the word 'kill' from the big Indian. But the other voice was definitely that of a white woman speaking English and gave Talon assurance that at least one of the captives was still alive. But he wondered, *Why are they staying here, what are they waiting for?* He determined to study the terrain of the plains before him and perhaps form a plan as to his approach for freeing the women. He backed away from the edge and began to glass the entire valley, each ravine, every pile of boulders, every cluster of trees, anything that would provide cover and a vantage point. He looked for a possible route to approach their camp undetected, and any trails that would lead away for an escape route. He looked and thought and considered. Exasperated, he stood and began to walk the perimeter of the butte for a more thorough look-over of the area. He also examined the surrounding rim-rock for any other way to descend the flat-top, but there was none.

Well, if they think I'm gone, they won't be expectin' me, maybe, but I can't take that chance. But if I at least come at 'em from a different direction, that'll give me a little advantage. He went to his horses, tightened the cinches and rigging, mounted up and started for the narrow trail. As he approached the steep slide, he dismounted and, taking the lead rope, stepped over the edge and dug in his heels to step and slide down the chute, coming to a rest at the bottom.

He looked up at his Grulla that was staring at him with head hanging over the declivity as if he was crazy, which he thought he was, at least a little. But he stepped back up the slide a few paces and tugged on the lead rope, as he said, "Come on boy, you can do it." As Dusty moved his hoof forward with a slight tremble, Talon stepped back ready to get out of the way and the horse came sliding down with his front legs braced before him, his hind legs under him and his rump dragging like an anchor. But he made it safely down. Talon led the horse away from the incline and started back up to retrieve the pack horse, still laden with the packs.

It was as if the pack horse had watched Dusty for an example and he did exactly as his friend, complete with the rump anchor slide. With both horses safe at the bottom of the slide, Talon went to the front of the pack and began to lead the two horses down the slide rock trail to the bottom. When the path leveled out and they were in the cover of the juniper, Talon took a few moments for a breather, then mounted up and started around the butte to make a circuit on the east side away from the Cheyenne camp.

He spotted a likely campsite from above that would suit him for the remainder of the day and would provide cover until he could scout out the camp of the Cheyenne from ground level. He would not attempt to reconnoiter in broad daylight, and definitely wouldn't try a rescue until under cover of darkness. So he would make a camp, tether his horses and wait at least until dusk before he started his reconnaissance of the Cheyenne camp. It would also give him time to thoroughly consider any plan and all possibilities. *Maybe even talk myself outta this craziness,* he thought. But he knew he would go forward because his Pa always told him, 'If it falls to you for the doin' of it, then get it done and don't be wastin' time waitin' for somebody else to do it for you.'

Early afternoon saw Talon dropping off the steep bank of the ravine that was thick with cedar and a few stunted willows in the bottom. From the top of the butte, he noticed the greenery in this ravine that told of the possibility of a spring and knew this would be a good location for a day-camp and it appeared to provide good cover and possibly some graze for the horses. If there was water, that would be a plus. When the Grulla cleared the brush and stepped to the bottom, his hoof sunk into the moist clay and pulled loose with a sucking noise that betrayed the moisture below. Talon looked up the ravine and saw the willows and green of the grass and knew they were in luck with a small spring that would enable them to refill the water bags and canteen, as well as give the horses ample drink. He dismounted, loosened the cinches and rigging and let the horses find the water and grass as he stepped into the shade of the twisted cedar and large juniper. Now he waited.

Chapter Thirteen

Stalk

SMOKEY LICKED TALON'S face to bring him awake and Talon knew that the dog was not warning him of any danger but just waking him up. Although the young man had his pistol and Bowie knife at hand, he was not alarmed and sat up to the grey light of dusk. The fading colors of the sunset were held loosely on the underside of the few clouds and Talon knew it was time for him to begin his scout of the Dog soldier camp. He checked his horses and saw they were contented with the grass and water nearby and knew they would not wander. He pulled his Henry repeater from its scabbard and with Smokey at his side started in the direction of the Cheyenne camp.

He could move as stealthily as any Indian and quieter than most. It was second-nature to him to pick his steps with his moccasin feet avoiding any loose stones, pine cones or branches that would be a giveaway. Moving in a crouch from tree to cholla cluster to sage or boulder, the fading light was enough for him to see but too dim to cast a shadow. As he neared the camp site, he dropped to his belly and hid himself behind a small sage. With nothing but cactus, sage and buffalo grass for cover, he knew he would have to move very slowly and do nothing that could be easily detected. The slight rise before him obscured him from the camp and likewise, the camp from him, but it would allow him to move closer. He also knew any lookout would be high enough to see over the rise.

Carefully, he moved just inches at a time, often moving nothing but his eyes to scan everything before stretching out an arm to pull himself along. Half an hour passed before he neared the crest and a small patch of prickly pear was before him. He was encouraged when he heard the shrill raspy trill of the cicada from the nearby junipers, knowing his movements had not startled them into silence. He worked his way around the cactus and slowly raised his head for his first glimpse of the camp. He could see no movement, there was no fire and there was no one talking. With it still early in the evening, he expected some to still be awake and moving around, but there was nothing.

He moved to the edge of the rise for a different vantage point and again peered over the rim into the campsite. There was nothing. Not a swish of a horse's tail, a step from a lookout, a sound from a captive, nothing. He waited and watched. Looking around at the cluster of juniper and back at the cliff side he was certain he was at the right location. He looked up at the escarpment where he was earlier in the day and back at the trees and overhang. Then he noticed the ring of stones where their cookfire had been, and the clearing between the trees where their horses had been tethered noticing the clumps of horse apples and he knew he had the right place, but they were gone.

He slowly rose looking around to ensure there was no one left behind to entrap him, and walked to the campsite examining every sign. He saw where the captives had been held, the bits of rawhide that had bound their legs and were cut so they could straddle the horses, and the tracks of the horses and moccasins of the Cheyenne. As near as he could tell with the darkness deepening, there were eight to ten Cheyenne with each of the captives doubling up with a warrior. The tracks led out to the east and could be followed, if the moon gave enough light. He quickly trotted back to the horses with Smokey at his heels. He tightened the cinches and rigging, mounted up and returned to the campsite to pick up the sign of the Cheyenne. He watched as Smokey sniffed out the tracks and then started off after them, Talon spurred his Grulla to follow.

It was not a full moon but the sky was well-lit with the Milky Way and a myriad of other stars and the half-moon rested as if cradled in the hands of the creator, sharing its light with the would-be rescuer. The horses kept a steady pace of a trot that pounded Talon's insides, but he was willing to endure the discomfort to gain on the Dog-soldiers.

It was evident that the Cheyenne had traveled after he spotted them from the flat-top while he rested the day away thinking they were still in camp. Now he traveled by night while they were probably sleeping comfortably. He slowed his pace, not wanting to come upon their camp unexpectedly.

They had cleared the hilly and rough terrain and were now in the flat but rolling grasslands. Talon knew they could be hidden in a low swale and he would be easily seen without any nearby cover. He decided to make for the first bit of cover and wait for daylight before continuing the pursuit. Within moments, he spotted a give-away of the top of a cottonwood that told of an arroyo that would shield him from sight. He stopped and watched for any movement, nudged his horse into a slow walk and approached the rift in the grassland. As he neared the slight drop-off he saw there was nothing but the one tangled cottonwood that was the sole reminder of a long-ago seep that held water. But it would do for his needs for the remainder of this night. As he dismounted, he looked around and saw no sign of recent visitors and after taking off the saddle and packs, he tethered the horses on a long lead and rolled out his blanket for a short rest. He would depend on Smokey and Dusty to give any warning, but he felt confident he could rest without interruption.

The morning light shone a muted gold from behind the low-lying clouds along the flat eastern horizon. Talon had shinnied up the snag of cottonwood and eyeballed the flat lands for any movement. Using his spyglass, he searched for any life besides the lazy tan and white antelope that watched from the low rising hillock in the distance. There was a small flat top with a formation of weathered grey stones that held his attention, but nothing moved. Beyond that unusual formation, about two hundred yards away was a scattering of grey rock that littered the small rise that stood as a lone sentinel upon which a lone antelope buck surveyed his domain.

If the Cheyenne were near, they were well-hidden. But Talon could only assume they had traveled further than expected or at least resumed their travel before first light. He dropped to the ground, quickly saddled Dusty and rigged the packs on the bay, mounted up and with Smokey again on the trail, resumed his pursuit.

Lone Eagle lay beside Two Bears as he pointed out the sod house standing near the corrals below them. "There are two men and one woman. They have guns and there are horses. You told us to find a place to trade, here you can trade. Or take them," said Lone Eagle.

"You will take the boy and see if they will trade. Three rifles and three horses for all the captives. If they agree, come back for the women."

The two men crawled back from the crest of the small rise, stood and returned to the horses and warriors. Two Bears ordered Little Antelope, "You take the women and go back to the ravine. Hold them there until we come for you." Then to Lone Eagle he said, "Take the boy, go to the white man and see if he will trade."

Little Antelope, with Ginny on his mount behind him, rode to another warrior and grabbed Mary Sue, dragging her from behind the man and dropping her to the ground. He laughed at her and swinging his leg over the neck of his horse, he dropped to the ground, grabbed Mary Sue by the hair and motioned for her to get on his horse in front of Ginny. He grabbed her leg and lifted her up as she struggled to straddle the horse with Ginny's help and finally settled herself. Antelope grabbed the lead line and trotted ahead of the horse to take the animal and women to a ravine about a hundred and fifty yards away.

Lone Eagle grabbed little Johnny from behind another warrior and laid him across his horse's withers in front of him and gigged his horse to start toward the sod hut and the corrals. He walked his horse around the slight rise and lifted his hand to the side with open palm forward. He slowly approached the hut, watching carefully. A man that was near the corral shouted and started running for the cabin waving his arms. Another man came from behind the cabin with a rifle in his hands and stepped back to the corner lifting the rifle as if ready to shoot, but he did not fire. The first man had gone into the cabin but now opened the door slightly and extended a rifle barrel through the crack. "What's he want, Fred?" came a crackly voice from within.

"Dunno, he ain't said nuthin'," answered Fred.

Lone Eagle continued his approach and little Johnny started squirming. The warrior slapped him on the rump and he immediately quit moving. The Cheyenne stopped his horse, grabbed Johnny by the hair and lifted his head making the boy squeal, and then said, "We trade."

"Trade? Whatchu mean, trade?" asked Fred.

"Trade boy, two women for three guns and three horses," proclaimed Lone Eagle.

"We ain't gonna trade. That's all the rifles and horses we got, we can't part with them. If we gave you all them, we'd have nuthin'! Nosir, we ain't gonna trade."

"No trade, we kill," said the Indian.

"But if we trade, then you'll kill us!"

"Please mister, they'll kill my sister and me if you don't trade, please mister," begged Johnny.

"Uhnuhnn, cain't do it! 'Sides, we already got one woman too many. No, you go on an' get outta here now!" shouted Fred and waved his rifle at the Indian.

Lone Eagle reined his horse around and started off but Jimmy started kicking and yelling. Lone Eagle kicked his horse to a gallop, grabbed Johnny by his hair and threw him to the ground causing him to bounce off a cluster of flat rock and lay still. When Fred saw the Indian's action he fired at the retreating Indian and missed, but Lone Eagle did not stop or even look back as he reined his horse around the slight rise that obscured the rest of the Cheyenne from view.

Talon stopped suddenly, knowing he'd heard a gunshot and that it wasn't too far distant. He scanned the area before him. It was the same rolling grasslands with little vegetation but to the east of him the terrain had a bit more variety, more hills and a few more trees.

He gigged his horse into a trot and told Smokey, "Move out boy, find 'em ,quick now," he instructed. The dog started his familiar ground-eating lope and stretched out away from his master. Within moments, the dog circled back and stopped Talon.

The young man took out his spyglass and surveyed the area, spotting a slight depression with some greenery and a rise behind it. It looked like the corner of a corral or something beyond, maybe the making of a ranch. He replaced the scope in the saddlebags and moved out slow and watchful. Then he heard more gunfire.

Once again he gigged his mount to a trot and nearing the depression he reined up and dropped to his feet, ground tying his horse and retrieving his Henry. He stealthily walked forward and peering over the edge of the ravine, spotted an Indian with the two women. Little Antelope was lying on the opposite bank trying to see the action at the ranch. His back was to Talon and the women, but the women were seated and tied together.

He started down the ravine, caught the attention of the girls and motioned for them to be quiet. He received a nod of their heads in response, then continued toward the Indian. As he neared the Cheyenne, he laid down his rifle and withdrew his tomahawk but before he was close enough to attack, Antelope turned and launched himself at the white man with a screaming war cry.

Talon was surprised and the impact from the Indian drove him to the ground but he caught the man's wrist with his hand and stopped the downswing of the knife. He bucked with his hips and threw the Indian from him, rolled over and drove his shoulder into his chest. The Indian kicked up and caught Talon in the groin throwing him aside as he struggled to his feet. Antelope raised his hawk and started his swing down but Talon kicked out at the Indian's leg and buckled it at the knee. When Antelope fell, Talon reared up on his knees and brought his hawk down to bury the blade in the forehead of the Indian splattering blood and brains on his hand and arm.

Without waiting, Talon jumped to his feet and ran to the women, cutting their ties and said, "Take the horses and go that way till you see my horses. Wait there for me, but if you see the Indians coming, take off!"

"They've got my brother!" proclaimed Mary Sue.

"Go!" ordered Talon.

The two women used hands and feet to scurry up the bank and out of sight. Talon retrieved his Henry and ran towards the gunfire. He saw the slight rise, ran up it and bellied down to a prone firing position. There was the body of one white man lying at the corner of the sod hut, but the shuttered window had a rifle barrel still giving the Indians battle. There appeared to be one Indian down, another off to the side but still mounted and holding his side as if wounded. The other five, two with rifles firing at the cabin, and three more were trying to get to the horses in the corral behind the cabin.

Talon had a clear field of fire and opened up on the three going for the horses. His first shot dropped one to the surprise of the others. But, with the other rifles firing they couldn't make out where his shot came from. Again; he fired and another would-be horse thief fell causing the third one to seek shelter behind the pile of logs with the other two Cheyenne.

Talon could see them motioning in his direction and he jacked another round in his Henry and let fly at the woodpile. He missed, but a chunk of wood flew up and startled one of the shooters. Just then, the door opened and the man from inside revealed himself thinking he could get a better shot, but instead he was cut down by Two Bears who was well hidden behind the woodpile. The man fell across the doorjamb and did not move.

The firing stopped as the Indians calculated their next move. To get to their horses they would have to reveal themselves. That's what Talon was waiting for so he jacked another round and watched. He forgot about the one that he thought was wounded and waiting off to the side of his horse, but he was reminded when a sudden jolt hit him in the back at the same time Smokey barked and he knew he had been hit with an arrow from behind.

He rolled to the side and saw the Indian notching another arrow but Talon quickly brought his Henry to bear and firing from his hip. His bullet hit the warrior in the chest where his arrow quiver strap crossed from his shoulder to his waist. The impact of the bullet knocked the Indian from his horse and when he hit the ground he lay still as his mount turned, looked at him and walked away.

Talon turned back in time to see the other three Dog soldiers fleeing on their horses leaving nothing but a rising cloud of dust. He looked at Smokey and said, "You could have warned me a little sooner, you know. Now, go get Dusty and those women. I think I'm gonna need some help."

Chapter Fourteen

Patching

THE WOMEN WERE SURPRISED to see the dog come running toward them without the man at his side, and when he started barking at them they didn't know what to do. Smokey took the lead rope from Dusty in his mouth and started off with the horse in tow, but when the women didn't follow, he dropped the lead and went back and started herding them like a couple of sheep until they finally started after the horses. "I think he wants us to come with him, Mary Sue," said Ginny, took the girl's hand in hers and said, "Come on."

When Smokey saw the girls moving, he retrieved the lead rope and started again in the direction of the rise where his master lay. As they neared the rise, the girls saw the still form of their rescuer lying near the top and started for him when Ginny said, "Be careful, Mary Sue, we don't know him and we don't know if the Indians are gone."

"I know, Ginny, but he's got an arrow in him and he needs our help," she said as she started running toward Talon. As she neared him, she heard him moan and saw him try to move but she stopped him with, "Lie still, you've got an arrow in you."

"Uh, yeah, I know. That's why I sent Smokey to get you. I'm gonna need some help gettin' it out. Think you can do that for me?" he asked as he watched her kneel beside him. Her expression was one of concern and fear, but also a hint of determination.

"We'll do what we can, but I've never had to take out an arrow before. Does it hurt?"

Talon couldn't help but chuckle a bit before he answered, "Well, it ain't the best feelin' I've ever had, that's for sure."

"Who are you, anyway? And, by the way, thanks for what you did. If you hadn't come along, they were gonna kill us. But let's talk about that later, what do we do to get this out?" Ginny had knelt on the other side of Talon and he looked from one to the other and at Smokey now lying at his feet.

"Well, it might be easier to do this in the cabin yonder, but you might need to check it out first. I don't think there's anybody left alive there, but maybe you can check. Just leave me here, but here," and he reached for his pistol and handed it to Mary Sue, "Take this, just in case. Do you know how to use it?"

"I think so, I have to cock it first, don't I?" she asked as she looked at the Remington .44.

"Yeah, but be sure to hold it with both hands, it'll kick a mite. I'm purty sure all the Indians are dead and I think those two men are too, but be careful anyway. You'll probably need to pull the one man outta the doorway and check out the inside. If there's some water, a place for some fire, and a bed of some kind, then we can work on this arrow in there. If not, we'll do it out here somewhere."

Mary Sue looked at Ginny and the two women stood to leave. Talon spoke to Smokey, "Go with 'em boy," then to the women, "He'll warn you of any danger and he'll help you too." They smiled and started down the slope. As they rounded the small hillock and the sod hut came into view, Mary Sue gasped as she saw the prone figure on the ground before her. She started running as she called, "Johnny, Johnny . . . Johnny!"

She slid to a stop and fell to her knees beside her brother and bent to touch his head. A large scrape across his forehead had swollen and turned varying shades of blue and purple, a cut on the side of his face had bled and covered his face with dried blood. His eyelids fluttered as he heard her voice but they did not come wide open. His breath came in ragged gasps but he was alive. Mary Sue lifted him to her and noticed his left arm bent at an awkward angle and knew it was broken. His pants were torn and revealed another wide, bloody scrape at the side of his knee. She started to cry and said between sobs, "You're alive, oh thank God, you're alive," as she rocked back and forth holding him close. Ginny was standing beside her and watching all around, fearful of any Indians or other peril but there was no movement and Smokey sat on his haunches waiting.

"Mary Sue, give me the pistol and I'll check out the cabin. You stay here with Johnny," instructed Ginny. Mary handed the pistol up to her friend as she nodded her head in agreement and watched her walk toward the cabin. As Ginny neared the soddy, she scanned the area noticing the bodies of two Indians and the man at the corner of the cabin and the one in the doorway. With one hand over her mouth and nose, she stepped over the body of the man and entered the cabin. Lying in the middle of the dirt floor was a woman, face down, but with blood over most of her back from an apparent gunshot wound.

Ginny gave a quick look around, noted a set of bunks with the lower one larger, a small cast-iron stove with a crooked chimney and what appeared to be a water barrel in the corner. A pair of shelves hung precariously from the wall and held a few cans, a bag of flour or cornmeal, and some tin cups. An overturned rickety table and three chairs had been pushed carelessly aside apparently during the attack. Everything about the place was dirty and an unpleasant smell permeated the place. Ginny was glad to get out and walked back to Mary Sue to ask about Johnny.

"I don't know, he's not coming around. I think this bump on his head hurt him somethin' awful."

"I'm goin' to get that other fella, and we'll see what we can do for 'em. Looks like we need to set up a hospital of some sort. That cabin yonder's gonna need some cleanin' for we can do much," said Ginny as she walked away.

When she returned to Talon's side he asked, "Where's the other'n?

"She found her little brother over there and she's tendin' to him," answered Ginny as she motioned in the direction of the others.

"Well good, is he hurt bad?"

"Dunno, he's scraped and bruised up, but he's not comin' round. He's still out of it. I think he hit his head pretty bad."

Talon reached out his hand for Ginny to help him up and received her arm and a lift up to his feet. He put his arm around her shoulders and she put her arm around his waist. He looked at her and said, "By the way, my name's Talon."

She smiled up at him and answered, "I'm Ginny and the other one is Mary Sue. Her brother is little Johnny."

"I know."

"You know? How do you know?"

"Your folks told me."

"You talked to my folks?" she asked excitedly, "When?"

"Just before I left to come after you."

"You mean you've been followin' us all this time?" she asked as they walked together nearing Mary Sue and Johnny.

"Yeah," he answered.

"Were my folks alright? I mean, the Indians didn't get them or anything; did they?"

"They were fine when I had dinner with them, but they were worried about you. The rest of the wagon train was trying to tell them there wasn't any hope and they should just go on without you, but . . ." and Talon let the thought drop without adding anymore for concern.

"Mary Sue, Talon here is the one that's been followin' us all along. He came from the wagon train!"

"Well, not from the wagon train, if you remember, I saw you in town in LaPorte."

Ginny stopped and looked at him and then to Mary Sue and laughed, "This is the guy we almost ran into on the boardwalk in LaPorte, remember?"

Mary Sue let a bit of a giggle escape and said, "Yes, I do remember. Surely that's not why you came, is it?"

"No, I didn't even know you were the same ones. I was ridin' Shotgun on the stage and we stopped by the train after the Cheyenne hit. We tried to get the troops from Camp Collins to come but they were gone elsewhere and nobody else would come, and it fell to me, so, here I am."

"Well, Mary Sue, we've got work to do before we can patch these boys up. Talon, how 'bout you sittin' here with Johnny and Mary Sue and I will get things ready and come back for the two of you. It won't take long. Come on, Mary Sue," she ordered and her friend dutifully followed.

Ginny took a rope from the saddle of Dusty and with Dusty to do the heavy work, they pulled the bodies of the two men and woman away from the sod cabin, and they drug them just far enough to get them out of the way so they could clean things up enough to tend to Talon and Johnny. There was one small shuttered window in the back of the cabin and one on the side near the corral. With both windows open and the door wide open, there was enough of a breeze to air things out and give enough light to start their work on the wounded. They carried Johnny in and placed him on the top bunk and returned for Talon. As they walked back to the cabin, he began giving them instructions for removing the arrow.

"Now, I checked it out, and you'll have to cut my shirt off, but be careful when you do cuz my Ma made it for me and I'd like to patch it back up. But the arrow didn't quite come all the way through, you can see here," and he pointed to the bump at the front of his shoulder just below the collar bone, "is the point of the arrowhead. What you'll need to do, is cut off the shaft, but not too close, and cut the muscle here at the point. Then you'll have to drive it through and pull it the rest of the way out."

Ginny interrupted him and said, "You want us to drive the arrow through your shoulder? How we gonna do that?"

"Well, you'll have to hit it with something. Maybe the butt of my pistol or something like that. But make sure you hit it square and hard the first time, cuz I don't think I could take too many practice shots," said Talon.

"Then after we push it through, what do we do?" asked Mary Sue.

"Did you say there's a stove in there?" asked Talon.

"Yes, there's a little one," said Ginny.

"Well, if there's a poker or something like that, before you start everything else, get the poker red hot and if there's any whiskey or something like that, when you push the arrow through, douse the hole with whiskey. Then you can cauterize the wound with the hot poker and that should do it."

"Well, you can tell us as we go along in case we forget something," said Ginny.

"Uh, I might not be able to," replied Talon.

"What? Oh, oh, you mean . . .oh, I wasn't thinking," said Ginny.

Talon lay face down on the lower bunk with his shoulder hanging off the bed and the arrow sticking up. Ginny sat beside him and prepared to start cutting on the shaft. She asked, "Are you ready now? This is gonna be hard for me. I've never done this before," she warned.

He chuckled a bit and said, "Neither have I, but go ahead."

The big Bowie had a razor-sharp blade, but was a little awkward in the small hands of the girl, but she soon prevailed and the shaft was cut through leaving about three inches protruding from the wound. The movement had caused the wound to resume bleeding but the shirt had been removed and the blood dripped to the floor. Talon rolled to his side to give access to the front of his shoulder so she could cut the flesh at the arrow point. She looked at Talon and at the protrusion and back at Talon and said, "O.K. now, here goes," as she touched the bump with the tip of the knife. She pushed down and pulled the blade across the protrusion, and Talon said, "Make another cut, like an X, to be sure."

She quickly complied and the blood flowed across his chest. He rolled back to his stomach and Ginny took a deep breath and looked at Mary Sue who sat in a chair near the stove with one hand on the poker as she watched the fire flaring in the stove. The girls nodded to one another and Ginny looked back at Talon's wound and said, "I'm gonna put the flat of the blade of your knife on the arrow shaft and hit it with the butt of your pistol. I think that will work best, what do you think?"

"Sound's reasonable. Did you find any whiskey or anything?"

"We're not sure what it is, but it smells awful, I think it's whiskey. It's in that brown jug there," she motioned to the floor near her foot. It was the typical jug used for corn liquor and Talon nodded his head and said, "Okay, whenever you're ready."

Ginny took a deep, almost sobbing breath and placed the flat of the knife blade over the arrow's shaft. With a couple of practice swings, she let fly and struck the blade and shaft firmly and drove the arrow down until the flat of the blade hit Talon's shoulder. She quickly bent to see the arrow protruding below his shoulder and grabbed the shaft, now slick with blood and pulled it straight down until it struck the hard-packed dirt floor and it was freed from his flesh.

Talon let loose a grunt that sounded like a bull moose at mating season and immediately lapsed into unconsciousness. Ginny grabbed the jug and poured the liquor into the wound at his back, then standing, she struggled to turn him over so she could put more of the foul liquid on the cut on the front of his shoulder.

With a grunt and a splash she succeeded and as she held him, Mary Sue put the hot poker into the hole and quickly extracted it as Talon unconsciously jerked away. Ginny dropped him back on his stomach and held him as Mary Sue again applied the hot poker. The rising smoke and stench of burning flesh gagged the women, but they forced themselves to roll Talon to his back and tried to make him comfortable. The two women staggered from the hut and leaned against the outside wall gasping for air and looked at one another in shocked amazement. "Did you ever think we'd be . . ." started Ginny only to be interrupted by Mary Sue with, "Never, never ever, in a million years. Now look at us. But thanks to that man in there, at least we're still alive."

Chapter Fifteen

Shame

TWO BEARS AND BROKEN nose rode side by side with Coyote following as they entered the village of the Cheyenne. Four days had passed since they left the sod hut ranch where the last of their warriors fell and now they must face what they expected to be the wrath of their chiefs. Led by White Antelope, Two Bears father, and Little Wolf, this village had allied with the village of Black Kettle and had signed the peace treaty at Fort Wise that severely limited the territory of the Cheyenne.

They were also allied with the Southern Arapaho under Little Raven and Niwot and were part of the smaller reserve that was located in Eastern Colorado territory between the Arkansas River and Sand Creek. Before this treaty, their territory encompassed the land from the Arkansas River to the North Platte River in Nebraska territory and the Dog Soldiers fought against this restriction and the limited territory for their people.

It was from this band that Two Bears and Broken Nose led a group of Dog Soldiers that disavowed the treaty and believed they must fight to regain their rights to hunt buffalo and live where they chose. The Dog Soldiers also believed the chiefs that signed the treaty did so without the approval of the rest of the tribe and without the blessing of the Council of 44, the supreme tribal authority. But now, Two Bears and Broken Nose were returning in shame and with the smell of defeat upon them.

While many of the people thought the Dog Soldiers would regain their rights, and hoped to one day join them in the fight, now the remnants of this band had ruined their hopes of a better life for the people.

As they entered the village, expectant faces looked for the rest of the war party only to be disappointed and when they saw the cast down looks of the men, the people turned their backs to them. Family members of the lost began to wail and throw rocks at the three men but they continued toward the center of the camp. The lodge of White Antelope would be in the center of the village and they must make their presence known to the chief. In addition, Two Bears must show himself before his father. The wailing of the women who lost their sons and assorted men alerted the chief and he lifted the buffalo calf hide from the opening to his lodge as he stepped out of the Tipi. He stood before his lodge and watched the three men approach, knowing his son was the leader of the Dog Soldier band that had left just more than one moon ago. There were fifteen warriors in the band that left and now only three returned.

When they neared the lodge of his father, Two Bears stopped his horse and dismounted. Broken Nose and Coyote dropped to the ground beside their mounts, as well. Two Bears greeted White Antelope, his father, with "My chief, we have returned and we have not done well. We hit the whites at their stage stations and a wagon train, but they fought fiercely and we lost many men. What you see is all that remains." He dropped his eyes from his father's and hung his head in shame.

"You did not bring back the bodies of your brothers?" asked White Antelope angrily.

"We could not, we would have died also," explained Two Bears.

"It is better to die bravely than to run away in shame," declared the chief. He looked at his son and his shoulders dropped visibly. He stood motionless for a moment, evidently in deep thought. Slowly he crossed his arms over his chest and turned away from his son to stand with his back before him. This was a sign of rejection- not only to his son but to a war leader of his people who was no longer welcome in the village, including those who rode with him. The crowd of villagers that had followed the three to the center clearing followed the example of their chief and everyone turned their back on the three men. Away from the crowd; the families of the lost warriors lifted their voices in mourning and wailed the loss of their loved ones.

The men were not allowed to enter any lodge nor retrieve any of their belongings. After they were gone, the villagers would divide their possessions among the families that lost loved ones. Now Two Bears, Broken Nose and Coyote were no longer members of this village nor would they be welcomed in any other village of the people. Although there were other bands of Dog Soldiers made up of Cheyenne and Lakota Sioux, even these bands were likely to reject them and not allow them to be a part of their bands.

Although the men expected this response, they hoped it might be otherwise, but when they were shunned anger rose within them and when Two Bears mounted his horse he dug his heels in and the three men charged from the village at a gallop, shouting their war cries.

He was determined to continue his fight and now, most of all, to get vengeance for the deaths of his warriors. These white men must pay and they would pay in blood. He screamed his declaration in a war cry as they rode from the village that was once his people. He would prove himself a greater warrior and leader than even his own father; his name would be spoken before the campfires and his deeds would be told for generations. They would know of Two Bears!

Two Bears and Broken Nose were armed with Hawken rifles and Coyote had a trade fusil that had a percussion action. Their supply of powder and balls was limited, at best, but all three still had their bows and an ample number of arrows. Two Bears wanted to return to the sod hut and the site of their last battle, but Broken Nose and Coyote said they wanted to find something to eat first and Broken Nose said, "We must hunt for meat before we seek vengeance. We do not know how many are still at that ranch and we grow weak with hunger. Let us find meat and rest and then decide."

Two Bears reluctantly agreed and the three men sought a camp near water and shelter. As dusk settled in, they came to the headwaters of a creek that ran away to the north and they knew would eventually run into the South Platte River. The willows in the bottom of the draw promised shelter and perhaps some graze for their horses, so the three renegades reined into the shallow ravine to prepare for the coming night.

As they tethered their horses, they agreed to take their bows and hunt both banks of the stream for game for their evening meal. Within a quarter hour, all three men were back in camp with a total of five jack rabbits and eager appetites. Quickly starting a fire, the three soon had the skinny carcasses on willow spits and crackling their juices into the fire.

After their satisfying meal, they sat back against nearby boulders and began to discuss their plans for the coming days. Two Bears was adamant in his desire for vengeance but the other two men were reluctant to return to the area that held so much blood of their warrior friends. Coyote suggested, "We should just go north and join the Lakota. They have not made peace with the whites and we can join them. Maybe get us a woman and make ready for winter."

Broken Nose nodded his head in agreement and added, "Yes, the Lakota have joined with our brothers in some of the

Dog Soldier bands and they are good warriors. as well. I hear they will never make peace with the whites. That is good."

Two Bears agreed with the thoughts of the Lakota but he growled as he said, "But our brothers' blood cries from the ground for vengeance."

"We do not know who brought their deaths. Did we not chase away the one that followed us? And surely the ones that killed our brothers at the stage station are not the same. How do we know who to attack or where?"

"Why should we care? We should kill all whites!" spat Two Bears as he kicked at the rocks before him. But Broken Nose and Coyote knew the one to blame was Two Bears and his anger that had caused him to make bad decisions when they fought the whites. He was their leader and he made the choices as to the time and place to fight, but his medicine had been bad. Broken Nose and Coyote looked at one another and both knew the other was thinking about the bad medicine they had followed. Perhaps it was time to make their own medicine.

When dawn brought the three renegades awake, Two Bears grumbled about not having anything left to eat from the night before and kicked at the still slumbering Coyote. Two Bears ordered, "You, Coyote, go hunting and bring us back some meat. Go, now!"

The smaller man grumbled as he rolled from his blanket and sought out his bow and quiver, Broken Nose looked at him and said, "I will go with you. Maybe together we can find something sooner." The two men retrieved their tethered horses and mounted up to climb to the top of the ravine's edge and follow the stream down the slight rise. When they were out of sight from Two Bears, Broken Nose said, "Maybe if we return to the village without him, they will let us back with the people."

Coyote looked at Broken Nose and with a questioning expression asked, "Have you known it to be done?"

"Yes, my father told of a time that warriors were allowed to return and only the leader was sent away. We only did what we were led to do and we fought well. We can try," he suggested. "If we take off now, we can be back at the village before the sun is high and he cannot follow us there."

In answer, Coyote reined his horse in the direction of the village and kicked him to a lope to distance himself from the angry Two Bears. Broken Nose followed close behind with a broad smile crossing his face.

Two hours brought the men closer to their village but they were surprised when they heard a considerable amount of gunfire. The village, numbering about seventy lodges, was situated on the south bank of Wild Horse Creek, in a slight depression below a long bluff.

Broken Nose and Coyote took cover to the north of the creek and watched as a large company of blue-coated cavalry attacked the village slaughtering everyone in their way. Women, children and old people as well as warriors were cut down and lodges set afire as screams and war cries rent the air.

The two renegades shielded behind a cluster of willows saw many of their people running across the shallow water of the spring runoff, fed creek and trying to find shelter among the willows and cottonwoods near the two renegades. When two cavalrymen followed, Broken Nose shot one from the saddle and Coyote drew down on the other, but the blue-coat turned and went back to the village before Coyote shot. Broken Nose quickly reloaded and waited, watching more of his people flee their village.

Broken Nose said to Coyote, "Follow me, we have to help them," and started across the stream. Coyote reluctantly followed the bigger warrior and held his rifle across his chest expecting to be cut down at any moment. As they neared the burning lodges, Nose saw another blue coat with a saber raised about to strike a fleeing woman and he brought up his Hawken and blew the man from his saddle. The woman saw the two warriors and ran to their side. Coyote said, "I will take her to cover," glad for the chance to get away.

97

Broken Nose stepped behind another lodge that smoldered but had not burned entirely and began to reload his Hawken. As he plunged the ramrod into the barrel he felt the hot iron of a bayonet pierce his back and he fell on his rifle into the smoldering lodge as blackness overwhelmed him. The last thing he heard was, "Yeah, I got me 'nother'n!"

Colonel John Chivington turned to his bugler and ordered, "Sound recall, we've done enough here. This was the honorable thing to do under God's heaven, to kill these Indians. Maybe we shoulda killed 'em all. But this is 'nough for now. Let's get outta here."

Chapter Sixteen

Healing

THE BIG HOUSE FLY buzzed around Talon's head and after several practice runs, finally landed on the side of the young man's nose. The snoozing Talon swatted at the fly and succeeded in waking himself up with the painful swat. "Ouch!" he declared as he felt the stabbing pain in his shoulder and the sting on the side of his face. He rolled to his side and looked around at the sparse furnishings of the sod hut, his movement causing the bunk above him to rattle and bring little Johnny awake. The boy groaned and asked, "Where am I? Ohhh, my head, it hurts!"

From the lower bunk came an unfamiliar voice as Talon said, "Well, glad to hear you're awake up there. Your sister's gonna be happy 'bout that."

Without stirring and causing more pain, Johnny weakly asked, "Who're you and where's Mary Sue? And Ginny?"

"I don't rightly know where they are, I just woke up my own self. But I'm Talon an' I'm guessin' the women folk are outside tendin' to the horses or gettin' us somethin' to eat. They'll probably be back in a bit."

"Wait a minute, what happened to the Indians? Where'd they go and how'd we get here?"

Talon chuckled at the boy's exasperation and said, "Well, some o' them Indians got themselves killed, and the rest of 'em run off. We found you right outside layin' on the rocks. So your sister brought you in here and put you on the bunk there and she's been takin' care of both of us."

"Well, what's the matter with you? Why are you layin' around?" asked the boy.

"One of your Indian friends shot an arrow into me. Your sister and Ginny took it out, but they weren't none too gentle so I'm layin' around tryin' to get over their rough treatment."

While he was talking with Johnny, Talon was surveying the cabin and its contents for his gear and whatever else that might be usable.

Standing in the corner next to the bunk were the Spencer and the Henry still in their scabbards. His saddle bags lay beside the rifles, his Bowie knife and scabbard across the top of the bags. To the side of the door were the packs and panniers from the pack horse and his bedroll lay atop the packs. It was evident the women had been busy inside the cabin as well, the floor had been swept smooth, the table and chairs sat against the far wall and everything else was neatly arranged and orderly. Although a mildly unpleasant odor lingered, the shutters were open on the windows and the door was ajar to let the air flow freely through and freshen the place up a bit.

The upper bunk squeaked as Johnny rolled to the side, but as he started to lean over, the doorway was filled with the return of the two women. Ginny had an armload of firewood and Mary Sue had a shirttail full of some kind of roots and Talon's pistol in her free hand. Noticing Talon was awake and looking at them Ginny said, "Well, it's about time. Course we got most of the work done while you've been takin' it easy but . . ."

She was interrupted by Johnny as he said, "Hi Mary Sue, Hi Ginny!" pushing himself up on his elbow to see over the side rail of the bunk.

"Johnny, you're awake!" proclaimed Mary Sue as she put the roots down on the table and rushed to the bunks to see her brother. Standing on tiptoes she reached to his face and asked, "How are you doing?"

"Well, my head hurts and so does my leg, but I guess I'm okay. Help me down, cuz I sure gotta go to the bushes!"

Both of the women laughed at the boy's insistence but realized he needed their help from the top bunk and Ginny dropped the firewood near the stove and aided Mary Sue as she lifted her brother down.

Talon said, "Hold on there boy, how 'bout come compny?" as he struggled to free himself from the confines of the bed. He was unsteady and the two helped each other as they stepped from the doorway and were struck by the brightness of the mid-day sun. As he shielded his eyes he turned in the doorway and asked the women, "How long were we out?"

Ginny answered, "You've been out since we took that arrow out yesterday and Johnny before that. You're both a couple of lazy no'counts," she kidded as they watched them round the corner of the hut to the path toward the privy.

When they returned, the women had rekindled the fire in the stove and Mary Sue was stirring something in a sizable pot that was smelling good to the hungry patients. Talon made his way to the bed and Johnny took a seat at the table. "So, whatcha cookin,' Mary Sue?"

"Well, we've got some good old fashioned rabbit stew going, Johnny. Ginny got us a rabbit and it's been cookin' a while, and we added some new cat-tail roots and we'll have some cornbread, so we should be eating high on the hog real soon," she declared with a smile.

Ginny, who was seated at the table opposite Johnny, looked at Talon and asked, "How's your shoulder feeling?"

"It's sore," he said as he moved his arm in a circular motion, "but I think it's gonna be fine soon enough."

"Well, you need to give it some more time to heal up before you try anything. But if you could show me a little about shooting your rifle I might be able to get us a deer or something better than a rabbit."

Talon looked at the two women and thought about the difference he noted between the two. Although he hadn't been around them long, it appeared Mary Sue was more at home at the stove while Ginny was more comfortable outside. He also saw the motherly way Mary Sue watched over her little brother and knew she was a woman bound to have a family and a home. But Ginny would be the type that would walk beside her man no matter where he went. He smiled at the thought and Ginny noticed his smile and asked, "What, don't you think I could shoot your rifle?"

"No, it's not that. I just noticed the two of you had found yourselves some trousers and you're lookin' more like you're suited for the frontier than you did when you were trippin' over your skirts."

Both women laughed and said, "We found 'em on those two dead farmers and thought they'd do us better than them. So we buried 'em in our skirts!"

"You didn't," said Talon with a grin. Shaking his head he added, "It's a good thing we don't believe like the Indians, 'cause if they're right, those boys are traipsin' all over the other side tryin' to explain why they're wearin' skirts!" Everyone shared a good laugh at the image of the men in the women's skirts.

"Serves 'em right!" said Johnny. "When that Indian offered to trade us for horses and guns, they said they wouldn't trade and didn't want us. The Indian said he'd kill us and they didn't care." His statement sobered the group and reminded them how close they all came to dying just a few days past.

Talon stood and went to the table to join the three and the discussion soon turned to what they should do in the next few days.

"We can't stay here, there's not enough supplies to last any time at all," declared Ginny.

"No, and I wouldn't be surprised to see those Indians try to come back for a little revenge. Maybe not, but we can't be too sure. Whenever someone needs to go outside, don't go alone and always go armed. I noticed you've been doin' that and that's good, just keep it up. I'm thinkin' I should be okay to travel by mornin' and there's enough horses for everybody so we should be alright. What kind of rifles did the men have that lived here?" asked Talon.

"Uh, the rifles are over there," said Ginny pointing to the wall behind the door. "We didn't find any pistols."

Talon looked at Johnny and asked the boy, "Could you bring one of those here, please?"

Johnny quickly jumped to bring the rifle. As Talon looked it over he noted it was a Springfield Model 1861 and wondered if the men had been deserters from the war. These rifles were the weapons used by the Northern forces during the war and weren't readily available in the West. Although some of the pilgrims on the wagon trains had them and other weapons from the war, most sought the repeaters like the Spencer and the Henry that Talon favored.

With the repeaters still difficult to obtain, Talon considered himself fortunate to have the rifles his father had ordered from a friend, Pierre Choteau. But the Springfield's would be usable by the women with a little instruction from Talon. They would need every rifle available when they sought to return to LaPorte and the stage station on the Cache La Poudre.

"Did you find any powder flasks or horns and what about lead or Minnie balls?" asked Talon as he looked at the women.

Ginny rose, fetched a large leather pouch and returned to the table. Inside were two powder flasks with a U.S. Army imprint, a larger canister of powder, two pouches of Minnie balls, a mold for the bullets, two bars of galena lead, and a canister of percussion caps. Talon looked up and smiled as he told the women, "Yeah, there's plenty here. We'll take some time this evenin' showin' you how to load and shoot these. You probably won't need to, but just in case, you might like to know what to do."

Both women nodded their heads in agreement but didn't make any comment.

"What about me? I can shoot too!" declared Johnny.

"Sure, I'll show you too, but as you already figgered out, these rifles are purty heavy. We'll just take it easy for now, you try shootin' one of these too soon, and you think your head hurts now . . ." said Talon as he left the boy to come to his own conclusion as to the pain.

Talon was surprised how quickly both women took to practice with the rifles. Ginny showed remarkable marksmanship, never missing the target but Mary Sure showed respectable results as well. He cautioned them all on loading, "Now, if you're loading and it's been a while since you shot your rifle, then it's okay to just use the valve on the flask to measure the powder, and put in right into the barrel. But if you just fired, like we just done, then put the powder in your palm and then down the barrel."

"Why do we have to do it that way?" asked Johnny, "wouldn't it be easier to just use the flask every time?"

"It might be easier, but if there's a smolderin' bit of patch or powder down there and that fresh powder hits it, then that flask'll blow up in your face. But if you just use your hand, all that'll happen is the powder in your hand will flare up. That'll hurt, but not near as bad as havin' the flask blow up."

"Oh, I see, yeah I guess you're right. That wouldn't be good," deducted Johnny.

The women chuckled at his response but the lesson was quickly learned. Talon was satisfied with their shooting and loading and also showed them how to use both his Henry and his Spencer but added, "I doubt you'll ever need to use them, but it's always good to know."

He didn't want to scare the women, but he wanted them to be prepared. But he also realized, they had already known what it was to be in constant fear of their lives when they were held captive by the Cheyenne. He hoped they would not have to face any more attacks by the Cheyenne or any of their allies but the uneasy feeling he carried was a familiar one and his Pa always told him to pay close attention to his instincts.

Talon surrendered his bunk to the women, which they shared, and he rolled his blankets on the floor before the door. He lay awake and considered all that had happened and what might yet happen. It was at least a four-day journey back to the Cache La Poudre no matter which way they chose to travel. If they returned on the same trail that brought them here, he knew it was nothing but wilderness and well-used trails by both the Cheyenne and the Arapaho.

Or they could go south and hit the Overland Stage Route that followed the South Platte River and hopefully catch a stage that would take them back to LaPorte. But he knew south was the direction the remaining Cheyenne Dog Soldiers had fled and he didn't know how far they would go or if they would be waiting for more warriors to join them so they could return to the ranch and re-claim their captives.

Chapter Seventeen

Vengeance

TWO BEARS LEANED BACK on his blankets as he watched Broken Nose and Coyote ride up the bank of the ravine. He grunted as he thought of them and considered their weakness when they always yielded to his threats and commands. He thought *That is why we lost our battles, with nothing but weak warriors how can a great chief defeat his enemies, Aiiiieeeee.*

He lay his head back and thought of the past several days. What he'd thought would be great victories, had turned into his shaming and being cast out of his tribe and family. He kicked at nothing in disgust and struck at the ground at his side in anger. He quickly sat up when he heard the sound of running horses. Grabbing his rifle, he ran to the edge of the ravine's bank and searched for any sign of attack but saw only a cloud of dust in the distance that appeared to be from fleeing horses. At first, he thought maybe Broken Nose and Coyote had startled some wild horses or even lost their own mounts, but then he had a sudden thought. "NO!"

He jumped up and looked at the disappearing cloud of dust that lay in the direction of the village where they were cast out.

Then he quickly turned to look along the bank of the ravine searching for any sign of his two fellow renegades. Seeing none, he whirled to look again in the direction of the village and realized he had been betrayed and his friends had returned to the village without him. He knew they might be accepted back without him, but only if they disavowed any allegiance to Two Bears.

His anger flared and he shouted again, "Aaaiiiieeeeeee! If I ever see you again, you are my enemy and I will hang your hair from my lance!" He turned and stomped down the side of the ravine to gather his few items and his horse to leave this place.

He jerked the head of his mount around and dug his heels into its ribs as he started up the side of the ravine. As he neared the top he heard a sound that was like thunder from the direction of the village. He stopped his mount and listened, it was a low rumble that continued, but was so far away it was unidentifiable. *Maybe a stampede of horses or buffalo or a rockslide in a canyon or something,* he thought and again jerked his horse's head around and dug in his heels. It was his way to take his anger out on anything or anyone within reach and right now it was his horse that suffered from his wrath.

As he thought about the rumbling noise, he thought about buffalo and his growling stomach reminded him of his hunger. *A fresh buffalo liver would be good for my strength and would be good medicine also,* he thought. The rolling flats south of the South Platte River were good buffalo country and was part of the reason the Indians were fighting to keep them. Many times, his people had wandered these plains as they followed the nomadic herds of the magnificent beasts of the plains.

But these vast herds had also attracted the white men that were hide hunters that took only the hides and left the rest of the beasts to waste. The thought of these white men fueled his simmering anger and he drove his mount to the highest promontory on the rim rock ridge that rose above the flats.

From there he could survey the prairie for great distances and if there were any buffalo herds, he would find them.

As he neared the jagged escarpment he stopped near a small cedar and tethered his mount. He made his way to the crest and lay prone on the flat rock that held the sun's warmth. Slowly, he searched the plains before him, careful to examine every ravine, every bunch of trees and cholla, the rolling hillocks and arroyos, and everywhere his eyes traveled, he watched for familiar shapes or movement. In the distance, about three miles away, a mass of brown slowly moved over a slight hillock and Two Bears knew it was a small herd of buffalo. Lazily grazing their way along the contours of the land, they were traveling where the greenest grasses told of moisture held by the snow drifts of winter and now nourished the luscious grass they sought. Two Bears grinned as he watched the herd slowly move in his direction. He looked carefully and mapped out his route that would intercept the herd and give him the opportunity to take a fresh supply of meat for the days to come.

Backing away from the crest, he gathered the lead on his mount, swung aboard and reined around to drop from the ridge and follow his selected route. It would take a short while to reach his chosen location and he wanted to remain out of sight of the herd. This was too good a turn of events for him to waste by being careless. He was almost to the site when he was alarmed by gunfire and it was nearby. He stopped his horse behind a thick juniper and dropped to the ground. His rifle in hand, he began to search for the source of the shooting and was alarmed when he recognized it came from three different locations. *There must be several and they're shooting at the buffalo!*

The loud reports told him these were buffalo hunters with their big guns and his anger flared. He ran back to his mount and retrieved his bow and quiver of arrows. He stopped and cautiously listened to mark where the shooters were and began to stealthily work his way toward the first. Within moments, he was behind the man and watched for a moment as the man laughed, loaded and shot with each bullet dropping another animal. The buffalo were milling about in confusion because the hunters were shooting from different locations.

Two Bears drew back the arrow to its full length, let it fly and watched as it was buried into the back of the white man leaving only the feather fletching protruding. The man's laughter was choked off as he gagged on his blood and fell to his face. Before the man's bulk hit the ground, Two Bears was trotting through the thickening dust cloud in the direction of the second shooter.

Although the first man's rifle had fallen silent, the other two men were paying little attention to anything but their own targets. Two Bears found a tall sage behind the second shooter and buried another arrow in his back with the same result as the first. When this rifle fell silent, the third man stopped his shooting and searched for his friend's location but the dust cloud from the milling buffalo prevented him from seeing any further than the nearest animals. He knew it would be useless to try to call for them as the bellowing of the big woolies would drown out even his loudest cries.

But this shooter was nearest the two hide wagons and the three men hired as skinners and he decided to go to the wagons to see if his partners had finished their shooting. He stood from his seat, grabbed his shooting tripod and turned to see Two Bears standing before him. He froze as Two Bears brought his tomahawk down and buried the blade in his forehead splattering blood across his face and back across the chest of the Indian.

The hunter didn't cry out but dropped his rifle and tripod then crumpled into a pile of blood and gore. The hunters had expected to be the only killers of buffalo this day and with the false security of their powerful Sharps buffalo rifles, they'd thought they were invincible. With blood lust generated by the killing of defenseless buffalo, the last thing they had expected was to be the hunted. On such premises of false security do many men lay down their lives.

Two Bears turned toward the wagons that were slightly obscured in the dust cloud and could barely make out two men on the first one and one on the second. He notched an arrow and let it fly to pierce the lower leg of one of the men on the first wagon. The scream from the wounded man alerted the others and with the shout of "Indians!" both the drivers whipped their horses into a gallop and left the area making almost as much dust as the buffalo herd.

Two Bears walked from victim to victim, he spat on each one and muttered, "These were nothing, there was no honor in killing them. Stupid white men that kill and waste the meat." He continued taking their scalps and gathering the plunder. Each man had a Sharp's rifle, Green River skinning knife, and some ammunition. However, the men had used most of the ammunition in their slaughter and the rest was in the wagons that were now many miles away.

With the shooting stopped, the herd started moving away and wouldn't stop until they came to water and graze some distance from the slaughter. Two Bears walked among the carcasses and shook his head in disgust. He stopped by a young bull and started to butcher the animal thinking about the fresh liver and the bile that would enhance the flavor.

As he rested on the haunches of the buffalo and dipped the liver in the bile, he considered the path he was now on. His vengeance was not just against the white man that killed his warriors. It was against all white men; but he would go in the direction of his last battle and if he saw more white men, he would kill them. If not, he would seek out the one that caused him to lose face and be expelled from his tribe. Then he would know the sweet taste of vengeance.

Chapter Eighteen

Preparation

"HEY, YOU BUNCH of sleepyheads! Come on and get outta bed, I could use some help. I shot us nice little buck and I could use some help gettin' it back here."

Mary Sue was busy near the stove with a pan full of thin-sliced salt pork and a pan of johnnycake. She laughed at her friend and the surprising announcement of her successful early morning hunt. Ginny had taken the Henry to try to get a better store of meat for their journey back to the settlement and her hunt had definitely proven successful. But her announcement didn't seem to rouse Talon who only stirred slightly and moaned with his uninjured arm laying across his forehead. Johnny was hopping down from the top bunk and looking at Talon, he said, "Hey Ginny, I think there's somethin' wrong with Talon. He don't look so good and he's sweatin' like he's hot or sumpin'."

Ginny propped the Henry in the corner and went to Talon's bedside to see the young man perspiring heavily and moaning incoherently. She looked to Mary Sue and said, "He's feverish and outta his head. I think his wound has got infected." She started pulling back the bandage. "Whew! It stinks too!" she said, making a face of disgust. "We're gonna have to open this up again, it looks like there's some pus drainin' but we need to clean it out 'fore it gets worse."

Mary Sue lifted the pans off the stove and wiping her hands on a rag she stepped to the bedside to examine the wound. Looking over Ginny's shoulder she agreed, "Oh my, you're right. We need to open that up. You'll have to cut away any dead flesh and clean it all out. Should we use that whiskey again or somethin' else?"

"I dunno, let me get started cleanin' it out. Can you bring me some cloths and some water? And I'm gonna need that smaller knife there on the counter, if it's sharp enough." Ginny had a sudden thought and said, "I'll be right back!" The she jumped up and ran out the door. In moments, she returned with a handful of what appeared to be a tangle of grey-green string.

When Johnny asked, "What's that for?" Ginny responded, "This is what folks call 'Old Man's Beard', it's a lichen that grows on tree branches, and is real good for puttin' on wounds like this. It takes out the poison and helps it to heal."

Mary Sue said, "Well, he's sure not gonna be in any shape to travel."

"You're right about that. Now… if he'll just hold still while I do this." She quickly cut away the beginnings of the scab, and with the fine point of the small knife, she dug into the wound and cut back the dead flesh exposing the pink healthy muscle. Dousing it with water, she dabbed at it with the cloth, sniffed at it and noticing the trickle of flesh blood, announced, "I think that's got it."

After rinsing off the lichen, she stuffed an ample amount into the wound and applied a fresh bandage. Soaking another cloth in the cool water she washed his face and his chest allowing the breeze from the open windows to cool him and help bring down his temperature. Talon had eased his struggling and moaning and appeared to rest better. Turning to Mary Sue, Ginny said, "I'm gonna take Johnny with me and get that deer meat before somethin' else gets it. We shouldn't be too long and then we can eat."

"Yeah, Mary Sue, you stay here and me'n Ginny'll get the meat," ordered Johnny as if he was the man of the house. Mary Sue grinned at her brother and replied, "Oh, yessir, master, I'll keep the home fires burning until the great hunters return." Although she tried to look serious, her face split with a smile and a giggle as she waved the two out the door.

The stream bed held a spring-fed creek no more than two feet wide, but it provided a constant source of water for the small ranch and for the animals of the plains. Just over a hundred yards from the cabin and with sporadic bunches of willows and stunted cottonwood was where Ginny had downed the buck as it came for an early morning drink. Ginny carried the Henry but she also had the Remington in its holster at her hip.

Johnny carried the big Bowie knife and one of the Green River knives from the cabin in preparation of the butchering task before them. The deer had fallen in a clump of Willows that overhung the small stream and stood taller than Johnny. The boy noticed some small game trails leading through the willows and looked for any sign of rabbits or other small animals. Ginny knelt beside the carcass and started the task of skinning and butchering. They would use the hide to bundle the de-boned meat and carry it back to the cabin.

"Come on Johnny, you can help with this," she instructed and as the boy knelt beside her, she showed him how to pull back the skin and run the edge of the knife between the meat and the hide to remove the skin as he pulled. The buck was small but meaty. The two worked tirelessly and soon had a pile of meat on the hide. As Ginny stood to look over their work and to search for a place for the remaining portion of the carcass, a movement back toward the cabin caught her eye.

Immediately she ducked down to hide behind the willows and motioned Johnny to be quiet and come to her side. As she watched, she saw a tethered pony at the far corner of the corral, out of sight of the cabin. Then she saw a crouched figure behind the corner of the corral that appeared to be watching the cabin. It was an Indian! Ginny caught her breath but carefully scanned the entire area, searching for any others and seeing none. Drawing deep breaths as she watched and thought about what to do, the figure started creeping toward the cabin. Ginny knew she had to do something before the Indian made it to the cabin and caught Mary Sue by surprise. Knowing Talon would be no help to her friend, Ginny realized she was the only hope for Mary Sue.

She motioned for Johnny to stay behind the willows and Ginny jacked a shell into the chamber of the Henry as quietly as she could, watched to see if the Indian heard but didn't see him hesitate or look around. She then stepped from behind the willows and started toward the cabin. The only cover between her and the Indian was a clump of sage about forty yards from the cabin and directly in line with her approach. She began to trot toward the sage keeping her eyes on the Indian and ready to stop and shoot. Just before she reached cover, she saw the Indian stop and turn her direction, he had heard her!

Ginny quickly dropped to one knee bringing the Henry up at the same time the Indian brought up his rifle in her direction. The roar that belched from the two rifles firing together sounded like a discharging cannon. Without realizing what she was doing, Ginny automatically jacked another round in the Henry but as she raised it back to her shoulder, there was no Indian!

She looked where he had been, saw a rifle on the ground and immediately searched the area spotting the fleeing Indian as he ran back to his horse. Before Ginny could take aim again, the man vaulted to his horse's back and lying low against the withers he fled towards the distant tree line at the far ravine.

What Ginny didn't see was when Two Bears fired his stolen Sharps rifle for the first time, he didn't expect the recoil of the big buffalo gun and was knocked flat on his back. In his shock and anger, his only thought was to flee before he was shot by his attacker and he left the Sharps behind in his haste and confusion.

Ginny stood to watch the disappearing cloud of dust behind the fleeing Indian and started back for Johnny and the meat. Mary Sue hollered out the window, "Are you alright? What happened?"

"I'll be back in a minute and fill you in," she called over her shoulder. She looked down at her free hand and saw it trembling. She tried to stop it but realized she was trembling all over as she walked back to the willows and Johnny. When she arrived, Johnny said, "Wow, Ginny! You almost got him, but you sure scared him. When he went down, I thought you'd killed him, but he sure got up an' took off."

They both laughed and Ginny grabbed the hide, handing the rifle to Johnny and said, "You protect the both of us till we get back to the cabin, okay?"

"Sure, I can do that!" he answered proudly as he put the rifle over his shoulder and pretended to march like a soldier.

After relating the details of the Indian and the shooting, the two women and Johnny had their breakfast and chuckled about the happenings. It was well after the meal before Ginny finally relaxed and the trembling stopped but she was still cautious and continually looking out the windows for any sign of other Indians.

Although they did their best to laugh at the way things had happened, they knew the danger was real and they were anxious to return to what they called civilization. Talon rested well for most of the day and by late afternoon he stirred and woke up, surprised at the lateness of the day. When he tried to sit up he winced at the pain and asked the women, who hadn't noticed he was awake, "What happened?" he asked.

The unexpected question startled the women and they looked at Talon. Ginny answered, "Your wound got infected and you were out of it. We had to re-dress it and you've been out most of the day."

Talon groaned and touched his shoulder, wincing again, and said, "It's sore, sure 'nuff."

He looked at the women and said, "Have you got somethin' to eat? I'm hungry!"

They smiled and got busy preparing another meal and while the women worked at the food preparation, Johnny piped in and said, "You shoulda seen Ginny! She almost killed that Indian and he took off an' left his rifle behind!"

"What Indian?" asked Talon with alarm written on his face.

Ginny went to his bedside and gave Talon the details of the confrontation ending with, "And that's the rifle he left behind," pointing to the Sharps in the corner. She lowered her voice so only Talon could hear and said, "There's something else, I didn't realize it right away, but after I saw his horse and I thought about it, I'm pretty sure he is the same one that took us from the wagon train. They called him Two Bears."

"That's not good. That means he's after vengeance and maybe wants to get you two women back. But he didn't have any others with him, so . . ." he lapsed into thought. He absentmindedly touched his wound, winced, and added, "I think we need to get outta here just as soon as we can." He struggled to get out of the bed and go to the table.

The four had become like a family and now discussed the need to be on the trail. Talon said, "We don't know if he's got any others with him nearby or not. But it's not worth taking any chances. Now, if we go back through the adobe hills the way we came, it will be a little longer but if we go south, that's also the direction of the Indians but it's closer to the stage route and we'd get back to the settlement sooner. I'm thinkin' we'd be better off goin' south."

The women looked at each other and Johnny said, "I'm with you, Talon, whatever you say is fine with me!"

Both Ginny and Mary Sue smiled, nodded, and Ginny said, "He's right. You know more about this country and the Indians too, so we're willing to do whatever you think is best."

Chapter Nineteen

Journey

WHEN THE BROAD BRUSH of the Creator painted the morning sky across the eastern horizon, wide bands of cloud glowed with muted pinks and oranges that cast their hue across the plains. The shoulders of the travelers caught the bent rays of the sun and basked in the warmth that gave a measure of comfort and security in this desolate land. The buffalo grass waved across the flats and obscured the arroyos that harbored the night beds of antelope and deer.

Five horses traveled single file without benefit of trail but bound in a southerly direction in search of the South Platte River and its companion, the road of the Overland Stage. The women were instructed to carry the big Springfield rifles across their legs behind the pommel and to keep them visible. With hats to cover their long hair and wearing trousers, Talon hoped the women would appear as men and give the small entourage the appearance of greater strength. He also had Johnny wear a large hat and carry the Henry.

The country they traversed was a flatland buffalo-grass prairie. With little variety, save the occasional rolling rises that dipped into shallow ravines and arroyos, they were readily visible at considerable distances. But their disadvantage was an equal advantage as they could also see any threat at that same distance, just as any possible attacker could drop into the small ravines to hide before attacking, Talon calculated they had the same advantage for protective cover. His eyes constantly roving, he let Dusty have his head and had Smokey continually roaming ahead in his usual sweeping motion searching for the scent of any possible threats. Talon knew his dog was not on a hunt for food but was on the look-out for Indians and he was comfortable with the ability of his four-legged friend that had repeatedly proven himself dependable.

Talon kept the greenery of a small meandering stream to his far right, knowing that stream would eventually search out the larger South Platte. But he was determined to bear due south to strike the Overland Trail and the stage line as soon as possible.

It was shortly after mid-day when they came to a shallow gulley with signs of water in the bottom. He motioned for the riders to pull up and water their horses in the small pool near the grassy flat and willows. Everyone stepped down and stretched their legs while Talon stepped to the slight bank and searched the prairie for any indication of life. Satisfied they were alone, he dug into the pack and handed out small handfuls of jerky and told everyone, "Loosen the cinches, and let your horses get a bite of that grass, we'll take a short break here, but not for long."

There was no shade but just being able to sit down on a solid seat, soft or not, was a welcome relief to the constant hip rocking gait of the horses. As Talon looked at the sky he commented, "I've been wonderin' 'bout those clouds to the southwest. They're lookin' purty dark and they're headin' thisaway. If the wind picks up or it starts to rainin', we're gonna have to find us some cover, but I think we've got a couple hours 'fore we have to worry 'bout it." The women looked at the sky and nodded their heads in agreement as they chewed on their jerky.

The small cavalcade covered several miles before the wind started throwing sand in their faces but they bowed their heads, pulled down their hat brims and upped on their collars to try to find cover. Talon had spotted a slight bluff to his left and farther south and they were slowly making their way against the rising winds.

He watched the clouds rolling and turning darker. Suddenly, a jagged shaft of lightning crackled through the blackness, startling the horses and riders, and giving the riders a few challenging moments trying to get them under control. But the storm was still several miles distant and they quickened their pace toward the bluff. As they neared the small mesa, Talon led the band to the lee side away from the billowing clouds. Spotting an overhang from a wide vein of flat sandstone he hollered, "Over there," as he pointed and reined his horse in that direction.

He quickly dismounted, tethered his horse at a cluster of juniper and pinion and tied off the pack horse. He quickly loosened the cinch and dropped the saddle and packs to the ground. Then he hurriedly grabbed the tarpaulin from the pack and went to the slight overhang. With the coil of rope, he secured the back side of the tarp to the stone, stretched it out and with the rope tied off to the nearby juniper, fashioned a reasonable shelter for the group.

While he was working on the shelter, Johnny and Mary Sue were gathering firewood and Ginny was tethering the rest of the horses to a picket line between the trees, giving the horses a windbreak between them.

By the time the group made it to the shelter, the wind was howling its protests and the clouds were letting loose their moisture. Talon drug the panniers to the sides of the shelter and stood the saddles on their pommels with the pads toward the inside on the opposite side. The blankets had been spread toward the back and the fire was starting to lick at the dry cedar and pinion branches the women had gathered.

Suddenly, a strong gust of wind flapped the tarp and threatened to take it, but Talon grabbed a corner and the rope to hold on and fight against the wind. Then the rattle of hail began to beat the ground, the tarp and the overhang as the ice balls bounced and danced like tiny white leprechauns showing their glee at the cornered quartet.

Ginny and Mary Sue huddled together and Mary Sue grabbed Johnny and pulled him close beside her while Smokey huddled at their feet. They watched as Talon clung to the corner of the tarp and ducked his head against the onslaught. The rain and hail were bouncing off his drooping hat and running down his back, but still he held on as Ginny wondered where he had the strength when she realized he was holding the rope with his wounded shoulder.

The storm raged and screamed as the wind whistled through the trees and around the bluff, relentlessly throwing hail from the clouds and mudballs from the bluff at the man that fought against them. The flames of the campfire danced and licked at the wood, drawing frightful images on the imagination of the women that gazed into the blaze. Their glassy stares looked like the frozen eyes of the dead; without movement or emotion. With their arms entangled and their blankets, the women resembled mummies. They had also removed their hats and the tangled mass of hair that fell past their shoulders added to the macabre appearance of the dancing shadows on the sandstone wall.

Talon was relieved when he felt the storm lose some of its force and he began to relax his hold on the tarp and rope but he waited a bit longer before releasing his grip. He turned to the women and they stirred as if awakened from a nightmare and smiled at the man who had rescued and now cared for them.

Ginny had allowed herself to entertain thoughts of the man that gave rise to speculation of a future together and she smiled at the remembrance and thought of the possibilities. The women had talked together about Talon and Mary Sue reminded Ginny that the two of them had vowed not to consider marriage until they reached Oregon. But Ginny argued that they were now alone and might not go to Oregon.

Mary Sue had smiled and said, "You're taken with him, aren't you?" to which Ginny replied, "Maybe," and both smiled at the thought.

Talon fed the hungry flames more wood and looked into the growing darkness toward the horses and said, "Well, ladies, I think the storm might let us have some of that deer meat for supper, if you're of a mind to wave it over the fire and warm it up a mite."

They unwrapped from the blankets, rose to their task and started preparing supper for the hungry travelers. Left-over johnnycake and freshly seared venison steaks made a fine feast as they sat around the now, slow-burning campfire. With the reflected heat from the sandstone wall and the crudely structured shelter, they found comfort and warmth for a good night's rest. Smokey stood guard duty as he slumbered next to Talon beside the coals of the fire.

Chapter Twenty

Adobe

THE BRIGHT BLUE SKY of early morning brought a cheerful start to the day. Talon allowed a leisurely beginning to give time for the early breeze and warm sun to do their work of drying the trail. When the women asked, he explained, "There's a lot of adobe clay in this area and when the rains do their work, it gets slicker'n snot on a brass door knob and that makes it a tad tricky for your horse to get good footing. There's been more'n one horse end up with a broken leg when they were slippin' and slidin' on that stuff."

"Oh, it surely can't be that bad, can it? Can't we just go around it or something?" asked Mary Sue.   Talon was busy taking down the tarp and gathering the packs. He turned and looked at the woman then turned around and said to Johnny, "Johnny, see that pile of rocks over yonder, just the over side of that little arroyo?" as he pointed in the direction of the rocks. It was a small pile near a big cholla cluster and lay just beyond a slight dip. The soil didn't appear any different than what was around them with random weeds, a single Indian Paintbrush struggling under one orange bloom, a small bunch of prickly pear. "How 'bout you running over there and fetch that little rock from the top and see if you can do it real quick without fallin' down?"

The boy looked at the stack of stones and back at Talon and took off running. Every step he took, the clay soil stuck to his boot soles and with each additional step the boots got heavier with the mud.

He had gone no more than fifteen feet when he started slipping and wind-milling his arms as his feet flew up in front of him and he landed on his rump. With his hands in the mud, he turned and looked at Talon, saying, "You still want that rock?"

The women were doing their best to stifle their laughter and looked from Johnny to Talon and Mary Sue said, "O.K., I understand. Now, will you help Johnny?"

Talon's long strides brought him to the side of the boy and he picked him up and carried him back to the camp. With the camp at the foot of the bluff and the sandstone outcroppings, the soil was more sand and gravel and did not have the problem of the slick adobe.

Mid-day saw them back on the trail to the south and bound for the Overland Trail. Talon led the lot and maintained his vigil of the surrounding flats, but he was uneasy. There was no sign of any danger, nothing that caused alarm, but the hairs on the nape of his neck continued to give warning. He tried to be as casual as possible and reined his mount slightly to the right toward a distant rise and cluster of pinion.

He continued his observation of the flats and watched for movement when he saw Smokey trotting back in his direction. The dog was repeatedly looking over his shoulder, but never wavered in his direction toward Talon. As the man watched, Smokey came alongside, circled behind the horse and trotting alongside, started growling and looking in a direction slightly left of their travel.

Talon turned and motioned the rest to follow him quickly. They kicked their horses to a canter and made for the draw by the pinion. When they dropped down into the shallow arroyo, they quickly dismounted and Talon said, "Stand by your horse and keep 'em quiet. There's somethin' comin' and Smokey's not happy about it. I'm gonna check it out so you stay here, but keep your rifles handy."

Talon ground-tied Dusty, slipped his Spencer from the scabbard and crouched below the edge of the rise. He then dropped to his knees, then to his belly to peer over the edge and scan the plains. He could see nothing. He returned to his horse and retrieved his spyglass and resumed his place of vigil. The flatlands showed no sign of life as he scanned everything before him. Turning to the side, he searched the distant flats and the occasional buttes and the rolling hills. Some distance away he spotted a grazing herd of antelope but there was no sign of alarm.

He turned and looked to the west and the distant juniper covered ridges showed nothing. Talon looked at Smokey who was now lying beside him and asked, "So, what'd you see boy? I ain't seein' nothin'."

Smokey was looking directly ahead to the southeast and growled. Talon raised the spyglass to his eye and looked again. Finally, he saw what had alarmed the dog. Less than two miles away and traveling in a due north direction was a band of Indians. As near as he could make out, they were Cheyenne and there were maybe thirty of them. He watched them for a moment before he turned to his companions and said, "There's a big party of Indians moving along over yonder. We're gonna have to stay here and keep quiet and hope they pass on by. Stay by your horses, talk to 'em and pet their heads and necks to keep 'em quiet. If they get a whiff of those Indian ponies and whinny to 'em, we'll have more trouble'n we need. Also, now would be a good time to pray."

Talon wasn't concerned about his own mount and pack horse, they had proven themselves many times before and he was confident they would keep silent. He looked at the sun and at the position of the Indians. He didn't want to have a reflection from his telescope give them warning and betray their location, but he wanted to keep a watch on them. With the sun slightly to the west, Talon turned his back to the bright orb and with his own shadow over the scope, he watched the slow progress of the Indians. While he watched, he prayed, *"Lord, we could sure use your help about now. If those Indians see us over here, we won't have a chance. So if you'll just let them go on 'bout their business, we'd sure be thankin' you. Oh, and by the way, Lord, these women could sure use a break. Could you work it out so we can get back to the settlement without gettin' killed. Thanks, Lord. Amen."*

What Talon didn't know about was the attack on the Cheyenne village by Colonel Chivington, and that was just one of several attacks and reprisals that would occur over the next few months as the outbreak of the Colorado Indian Wars gained momentum. These Indians were from that same village and were the spearhead of the attacks they felt necessary to show the white man they would not be destroyed nor have their lands stolen from them. Although the attack by Chivington was deadly and resulted in almost thirty deaths, it would not be the last nor the deadliest by the forces mustered by governor Evans of Colorado territory, and his primary enforcer, Colonel Chivington.

While they watched and waited, the Indians continued on their northerly path and bypassed Talon and company. When he turned to tell his companions the danger was past, they dropped to the ground and with deep breaths showed their relief. "How many were there?" asked Ginny.

"Oh, 'bout thirty or so, looked like they were a war party. Their ponies were painted and they carried their war lances. If they were just hunting, there woulda been fewer of 'em and probably wouldn't have lances. Somethin' musta got 'em riled up."

Talon replaced his Spencer and his spyglass and told the rest to mount up so they could make some time and put some country between them and the Indians. With the days getting longer, Talon was optimistic they would gain several more miles before making camp for the night.

Although Talon had never been in this part of the territory, he had spoken with Mac about it and knew the streams north of the Platte ran in a southeasterly direction before intersecting with the Platte. As dusk settled over the prairie, Talon noticed some cottonwood in the distance and realized they were nearing a stream. He thought to himself, *I sure hope this is Wildcat Creek. Mac said it was the last creek before he hit Bijou station and as near as I can figger it, that should be near-abouts where we are.*

Everyone was relieved to see the cottonwoods and the willows that told of a decent-sized creek and the possibility of a good campsite. Talon spurred his mount ahead to make sure there was nothing lurking in the copse that might be a danger and was relieved to see Smokey emerge with a broad smile and wagging tail. Talon turned in his saddle and waved the rest on and he began to search for a good flat campsite with some graze for the horses and shelter for the group.

It didn't take long for everyone to complete their assigned tasks of setting up camp and the horses were tethered by the creek bank with ample lead for water and graze. Gear had been arranged by the big trees and bedrolls rolled out on the thick bed of leaves. Mary Sue was humming as she busied herself with Dutch-oven, corn bread biscuits, and Ginny had speared several slices of venison and was hanging them over the fire on willow skewers. Talon and Johnny were giving the horses a rub-down with handfuls of grass and Smokey was lying beside Ginny hoping for a hand-out. It was a peaceful scene and as Talon looked at the camp gathering, he thought of family. He had admired Ginny and the way she seemed to respond to every challenge, and he also liked the way she looked. *She's easy on the eyes, that's for sure. I wonder if her folks left with the wagon train or if they went back to LaPorte? Guess we'll find out soon enough.* He was reminded of his home and his brother Tyrell, and wondered how he and

Elizabeth were doing, knowing they would be busy with all the spring chores of the ranch with calving and taking care of the cattle. Although it was not unusual, young men the age of Tyrell and Talon seldom got married before their lives were established with a home and all, but there were always exceptions. *Are you crazy?* He thought, admonishing himself, *You hardly know the girl and this ain't no time to be thinkin' about marriage!*

He turned back and busied himself with the rubdown and focused on the work before him. The women soon called them to supper and Johnny said, "Bet I can beat you, Talon!" and took off at a run. Talon chuckled and made as if he was racing the youngster and followed him to the campfire. Seated around the fire, the group shared a prayer of thanksgiving and started their meal. While they ate, Ginny asked, "Talon, you seem to be pretty comfortable with praying, are you a Christian?"

Talon took a sip of his coffee and looked up at the woman and asked, "Well, Ginny, I guess I'd have to ask you just what you mean by being a Christian?"

"I mean, do you believe in God?"

Talon smiled and said, "Yes, I believe in God. But would it surprise you that most Indians believe in God? However, they often call Him; Creator, or Great Spirit, or Manitou, or perhaps other names, but they believe in God. So, would you call them Christian?"

A confused look crossed her face as she responded, "Uh, I didn't know that, and no, I guess I wouldn't call them Christian."

"You see, Ginny, I believe the Bible teaches that being a Christian is a way of life that begins when you accept Christ as your personal Savior. The Bible says in James 2:19 'the devils believe and they tremble' so it's not just believing in God, you must accept Christ's sacrifice on the cross and believe He died to save you and receive Him as your Savior. When you do that, God gives you eternal life and you are a new creation like it says in II Corinthians 5:17. That's what makes a Christian.

Have you done that, Ginny?" asked Talon as he took another bite of venison and washed it down with coffee while he waited for her answer.

"Uh, well, I always thought I was a Christian because I went to church with my family, but no, I don't think I've ever done that," she said rather timidly. She was surprised at Talon's confidence as he spoke about his faith and she knew she didn't have that. Her life had been one of just being a good person thinking that was what it meant to be a Christian and she had never been confronted with this simple, but profound truth. She looked at Mary Sue and saw her friend smiling at her with love and concern as if she knew all along that her friend needed more in her life.

"If you'd like to make sure of Heaven and receive Christ as your Savior, we can do that right now, Ginny. It's as simple as asking God for his free gift of eternal life and seeking his forgiveness for your sins. Just a simple prayer in your own words between you and Him and He will give you that gift. I think Mary Sue would be happy to pray with you, if you want."

Ginny looked at Mary Sue and her friend nodded and reached out her hand to clasp Ginny's. The two women bowed their head and prayed quietly together. When they said "Amen" together, Ginny lifted her head and wiped tears from her eyes and smiled at Talon as she said, "Thank you, now I know for sure I'm a Christian!" There were smiles all around and the meal was soon finished and everyone turned in for a good night of peaceful sleep.

Chapter Twenty-One

Bijou

WHEN MORNING GREETED the group of travelers camped in the cottonwoods, the campsite was busy with preparations to travel. All that remained at the cook fire was the coffee pot and the cups that sat on the nearby stones. The horses had been brought to the camp from the creek-side and stood waiting as Talon and Johnny worked at saddling the mounts and rigging the pack horse. Johnny asked, "Why is it those women think they gotta be takin' a bath anyway? You 'n me have been on the same trail an' we ain't worried about a little dust an' dirt."

Talon chuckled and said, "Well Johnny, from what I understand about women is you don't understand women. See, us men just see things kinda simple like, but women now, they gotta complicate everything just to confuse us men. What they don't seem to know is we're already confused and they don't need to do any more confusin'."

Johnny shook his head in consternation as he answered, "I'm confused."

"Me, too," shared Talon as he tightened the last cinch. "Let's go have another cup of coffee 'fore we pack up the coffee pot and maybe the women'll be ready by then."

While they sat and watched, the two women walked from the creek, laughing and running their hands through their hair. Seeing Talon and Johnny looking at them, Ginny said, "Well, ain't we pretty now that we're all clean?" She struck a pose and was copied by Mary Sue as they waited for the response of the two coffee drinkers. Talon poked Johnny with his elbow and said, "I dunno, whatdaya think Johnny, are they pretty or not?"

"As my Pa used to say, they're prettier'n a new-born colt, and just as wet too!" With everyone laughing they made their way to the horses and were soon mounted and back on the trail. The mood was cheerful and the group even started singing together, although Talon's voice did not lend to the musical part of the journey. The women enjoyed harmonizing on the song, Wait for the Wagon, as Mary Sue started off with,

Will you come with me, my Phillis dear, to yon blue mountain free,

Where the blossoms smell the sweetest, come rove along with me.

Ginny picked it up with,

It's every Sunday morning when I am by your side,

We'll jump into the wagon, and all take a ride.

Talon and Johnny lent their voices, such as they were, on the chorus,

Wait for the wagon, Wait for the wagon, Wait for the wagon and we'll all take a ride.

Everyone laughed and the cheerful mood continued with constant chatter as they now rode side by side and two by two. Talon and Johnny in the lead were the first to spot the tell-tale sign of greenery that was a give-away for the South Platte River. The terrain had changed considerably and their view of the line of trees was broken by several small buttes and ridges that told of other channels carved by the river in years' past.

Talon knew they would have to find a safe crossing to reach the stage road on the south bank but he was also aware of the South Platte's reputation for quicksand and he wasn't too anxious to try his hand at the crossing, but he knew it would be necessary.

The group of riders now rode single file as they dropped off the ridge to the riparian flats and made their way through the willows and cottonwoods. Closer to the uplift at the ridges grew Boxelder and Maple in thick woods where deer made their beds and Talon saw four doe tiptoeing away from the intruders.

As they neared the riverbank Talon told the others to wait while he checked for a crossing and they happily dismounted to stretch their tired legs. Ginny took the lead rope of Talon's pack horse while he rode the bank and scanned the river bottom. The water was still somewhat murky with the snowmelt of the high mountains bringing the silt from the feeder streams into the main channel.

When he saw what he thought would be a good crossing point, he gigged his mount down the bank and into the water. Carefully leaning over the withers of his horse, Talon looked for the gravely bottom on the riverbed. With the South Platte being a rather shallow river, the water never reached the bottom of his stirrups and even through the murky waters he could see the bottom. Carefully watching the current, he slowly moved his mount across the stream. As he neared the far bank he saw a swirling eddy slightly downstream and reined his mount upstream to avoid it and easily made the bank. No sooner than horse and rider were out of the water, the mount did his shaking belly roll that rattled gear and rider alike. Talon walked his mount along the bank and downstream to get a better look at the swirling eddy and saw that the semblance of a whirlpool was actually a trap of quicksand.

After crossing back to join his comrades, Talon pointed out the crossing and the landmark tree on the opposite side to use as their guide. Then he said, "Ginny, I'm gonna have you lead out, but be very careful as you near the far bank. There's an eddy just downstream so you'll have to point your horse upstream from there so you'll miss the quicksand. I'll follow behind to make sure everybody gets across without any trouble. You can lead out alright, can't you?" he asked.

"I guess so, it don't look too hard. I think we can make it alright," she answered as she mounted up. The others followed suit and Ginny and her mount were soon in the water.

Talon had told them to space out and take their time, giving the horses their heads and letting them find their own footing. Ginny was half way across when Talon spurred his mount into the water. He stood in his stirrups and watched the line of riders and was pleased with their progress. He caught something out of the corner of his eye and looked upstream to see a snag of a tree that had been uprooted in the recent storm, floating with the current and headed straight for the line of riders.

Talon hollered a warning, "Look out! There's a tree coming, move out!" But the splashing of the horses against the current and the squeak of the gear and noises of the river made it impossible for the women to hear his warning. Johnny heard him holler and turned in his saddle to see what he wanted and Talon successfully warned him with gestures and shouting. Johnny reined up his mount thinking the tree would pass in front of him and Talon came alongside. They watched helplessly as the tree rolled and tumbled with the current and slowly moved in the direction of Mary Sue's horse. But the women continued their crossing unaware of the new danger. Their eyes were on the far bank and watching for the dreaded quicksand pool.

As Talon and Johnny remained in the river watching the women, they saw Ginny's mount rising out of the water and Mary Sue approaching the upstream side of the eddy and the quicksand. Suddenly, the long branches of the current riding tree scraped the rump of the Mary Sue's mount and startled the animal that twisted around to see what new danger now

132

threatened. Mary Sue grabbed the horn and pulled the reins taut trying to control the frightened animal as the horse began to thrash in the water. The woman dug in her heels and pulled on the reins to bring the animal's head back to face the far shore and as she hollered and kicked, the animal took several hops through the current and made the bank and scrambled out of the water. Not realizing how close she came to death, the woman burst out in laughter as the horses shook repeatedly trying to rid themselves of the excess water.

When Talon and Johnny joined the women on the bank, Johnny was the first to speak when he said, "Boy Mary Sue, you sure looked like you were gonna get dunked but you handled that horse just like you knew what you were doin'!"

She laughed as she said, "I was just so scared and wanting to get to shore I had to make him do what I wanted and he did."

"Well, we don't have any time to waste and I don't know when a stage will be comin' so let's get up there to the roadway and see where we need to go," said Talon as he spurred his horse toward the roadway. The stage line road, also known as the Overland Stage Road, followed the South Platte from Julesburg to Latham where it was joined by the Cache La Poudre river. The stage road then followed the Cache La Poudre to LaPorte, which was the group's destination. When they came to the road, Talon stood in his stirrups and looked both east and west to see if he could tell where the nearest station was without success. He turned to the others and said, "Well, since we'll be goin' west anyway, let's follow the road that-a-way and if we come to a station before the stage gets here, we'll just wait at the station for the stage."

"If we're gonna take the stage, what're we gonna do with the horses?" asked Johnny.

"I figger to take mine with us, but those three we'll probably trade for the stage fare," explained Talon. Johnny reached down and patted his horse's neck and said, "I was just getting' used to ol' Rusty here. Me an' him are kinda pals."

Talon smiled and understanding the connection between a man and his horse, said, "Well, Johnny, we'll just have to take it one day at a time. If it can be worked out for you to keep him, then maybe. But ya' might be thinkin' 'bout what your Ma might have in mind for you."

"Yeah, I forgot about that. Ya think she's gonna be alright? My Ma, I mean. You said she had been hit by an Indian arrow."

"The doctor that was takin' care of her said he thought she'd be okay and if she's like you and your sister, I'm sure it'd take more'n one ol' arrow to do her in," encouraged Talon.

The group traveled on the roadway riding two by two and remained watchful for any sign of danger. They knew they were still in Indian country and the possibility of attack was very real. Although the stage stations were about fifteen miles apart, there were few signs of any other settlement.

Most of this country was only suitable for ranching and it required a lot of country to support any sizable herd of cattle which made ranches few and far between. Although the bottom land near the South Platte would be suitable for farming, there were few families willing to brave the wilderness and the Indians to try to settle the area and establish a farm. Talon spotted what appeared to be a streambed that led to the South Platte and just past the small stream, a building. He pointed it out to the others saying, "Looks like there's a station yonder. We'll wait there for the stage."

Chapter Twenty-Two

Stage

THE DIM LIGHT OF EARLY morning separated the distant horizon from the darkness with a curtain of grey that made the far away bluffs dance like silhouettes with low-lying fog masking its features. Talon peered through narrow slits from his bedroll in the loft of the barn and forced himself awake.

Looking around, he saw the small figure of Johnny wrapped like a mummy in his blanket and huddled in a hump of hay. Talon sat up and looked around the empty barn and out the loft to the nearby cabin and the crowded corral below. He spotted his Grulla and pack-horse among the relief teams and the three mounts of his companions, noted his saddle on the top rail of the corral and the packs on the ground below.

Everything was just as he'd left it the night before and he reviewed the events of the evening as he rolled his blankets together. He remembered seeing Mac, the stage driver from LaPorte, and him saying he was the relief driver that would take the stage on to LaPorte and beyond. Talon smiled at the memory of the crusty old-timer and chuckled at his insistence that he ride shotgun for him. The women spent the night in the station and Mac had the bunk in the room below that was reserved for the relief drivers. Talon looked below and saw Mac emerging from the room and hollered, "Mornin,' Mac! Do you sleep in like this every mornin'?"

"Ever' time I can, you little pipsqueak! An' I don't see you at the breakfast table yet!"

"I'm comin', don'tchu worry, I ain't about to miss breakfast," answered Talon as he nudged Johnny with his boot to roust the youngster. As the boy stretched and rubbed his eyes Talon said, "I'm goin' to breakfast, and if you don't wanna miss out, you better hurry up an' join us!"

"Ummmhummmm, I'm comin'," he mumbled as he watched Talon descend from the loft.

The men were welcomed into the station by the women, already seated at the long table and waiting for them, with a cheery "Hello, sleepyheads!" and a giggle from both women.

The meal of biscuits, gravy and thin sliced venison steaks, was served by the wife of the station keeper, Elias Worthern. He joined them for the meal and when Talon asked if he'd had any Indian trouble, he responded, "Not directly. A couple of stages have been hit and we had one totally burnt and the horse stole. Course they killed everbody with it, but that's been a couple of weeks ago. But I heard about ol' Chivington attackin' a Cheyenne village east of here and I'm guessin' they're purty riled up about it, so I wouldn't be surprised if we had some more problems."

"I thought them soljer boys was 'sposed to be protectin' the stages an' such, not attackin' the villages," said Mac.

"From what I hear from roun' Denver City way is Gov'nor Evans and Chivington wanna get rid of all the Injuns. Now, just how they gonna do that, I dunno, but so far I don't like it. All they're a doin' is causin' us more trouble," observed Worthern.

His wife, Mamie, chimed in with, "And they ain't done nuthin' to protect us, neither. Why, if them Injuns attacked us, there's just us and the hostler an' whoever happen to be here to defend this here station. I tell you, I'm gettin' plum skeered," she commented while continuing with her serving.

Ginny and Mary Sue looked at one another and Mary Sue said, "Well, I'm glad we're gonna be leaving. I can't wait to get to LaPorte and see my Mama."

Ginny nodded her head in agreement as she forked a bite of biscuits and gravy to her mouth. Johnny came in and plopped in the chair next to Mary Sue and looked at everyone and asked, "So, you'all talkin' 'bout Injuns again?"

"Yeah, we were. And I was just tellin' Mac here about you bein' quite the Indian fighter too and how you took on ol' Two Bears and his whole bunch and run 'em off," said Talon with a grin. Johnny looked at him seriously and said, "Now Talon, you know I didn't do that all by myself. Smokey out yonder helped." Everyone laughed and helped Johnny fill his plate for his breakfast.

Talon had spoken to Elias Worthern about passage for the women and Johnny in exchange for the horses and although hesitant, he agreed. He said, "Them horses won't do me too much good. From here goin' west we use horses, but goin' east we use mules, on account o' the sandy soil an' the mules pullin' better. But the horses you got ain't big 'nuff for pullin' but I guess we can probly trade 'em off."

Most stage stations doubled as trading posts and social centers for the ranchers and farmers in the area and the many passers-by on the increasing number of wagon trains. Bijou was a hub of activity with more settlers coming and settling to the West of the junction where the station was located. However, it was also subject to more Indian attacks because the terrain provided more cover and there were more targets providing greater plunder.

It was mid-morning before the west-bound stage arrived and the group was happy to learn the stage was not over loaded and there would be plenty of room for all. Mac had asked Talon to serve as his Shotgun at least until LaPorte and he agreed allowing the Shotgun that rode in from Julesburg to have a relief and stay at Bijou to return to Julesburg on the east-bound stage. He remarked, "Suits me, what with them Cheyenne all stirred up an' the 'rapahos too, I'd just as soon stay to the flats where we can see 'em comin'!"

Talon climbed to his familiar seat, placing his Henry by his right leg with the bull whip coiled and hanging from the stock. The Spencer was strapped to the rail behind him and within easy reach while the two Springfield's used by the women lay alongside. The big Springfield's were too cumbersome to be comfortable with the women inside the coach.

Smokey took his familiar spot on top and just behind his master. Talon leaned over to watch the women and Johnny climb aboard and said, "Ladies, make yourselves comfortable. You pretty much have the coach to yourselves with only one other passenger, so far. But you'll probably find it more comfortable than the saddles you been forkin' the last few days." Johnny had asked to ride up top but Talon encouraged him to sit with the women and 'protect 'em' if they need it and he begrudgingly agreed.

When the coach rocked with the weight of Mac climbing aboard, Talon turned to watch the whiskery face of his friend appear over the seat on the box. He dropped into his seat and picked up the lines with his foot naturally going to the brake lever. He leaned over and said, "Ever'body ready? We're pullin' out!" and with no response from the passengers, he released the brake and slapped the team with the lines, rocking the coach back on the thorough braces and causing the team to lean into their traces and pull the coach away from the station. He started his usual commentary to continue the education of his Shotgun with, "We got a purty good pull up to the top of that flat-top yonder, but it'll be purty good goin' for a while thar."

He turned to look at Talon and said, "Boy, it shore is good to lay eyes on you. When you took off after them Cheyenne what took them women, I weren't sure I'd ever see you agin, an' here you are an with the women too, boy howdy, ain't that sumpin', yessiree." His grin parted his whiskers making his face look like the worn end of a widow's broom but Talon was pleased with the remark and chuckled.

"To tell the truth, there was a time or two I wasn't too sure my own self."

"So, whatcha gonna do wid 'em nowcha got 'em?" asked Mac.

"Whatdaya mean?" queried Talon as he looked askance to the old man.

"Wal, you rescued 'em so now yore purty much stuck wid 'em."

"But, but, Mary Sue and Johnny, they got their Ma in LaPorte, don't they?"

Mac shook his head and looked sideways to the young man as he said a bit more quietly, "Nah, she up and died. Guess them arrows she took an' losin' her husband and kids musta done her in and she just gave up the ghost."

"Boy, that's gonna be tough. They've been thinkin' all along that their Ma's waitin' on 'em. Now what're they gonna do?" Then he looked like he had an idea and he asked Mac, "What about Ginny's folks, did they stick around?"

Mac just shook his head and said, "They left with the wagon train. I think all them pilgrims figgered there weren't no chance o' them young'uns ever comin' back."

Talon took a deep breath and let his shoulders drop as he thought of the complications Mac just laid on him. He watched as the Jehu slapped the team with the leads and maneuvered them up the narrow trail that crossed the face of the ridge as they climbed to the top. Talon looked back to the disappearing station and the winding South Platte now partially obscured with the trees and rolling riparian flats below. He looked back and saw the rumps of his Grulla and the pack horse as they followed behind the coach on their short tethers.

"I tell you what, younker, I got an idee that might be an answer for you. I got a cabin, ain't much, just a couple rooms, back up in the Cache La Poudre canyon. Ain't too far an' it's in a real purty place. I ain't been usin' it, an' since my woman's been talkin' 'bout me quittin' drivin' and us goin' back to St. Louie, I won't be needin' it. If you want it, it's your'n."

"Your woman? Since when do you have a woman? You never told me 'bout no woman!" declared Talon with surprise.

"Well, course I got a woman. She's a widow lady that's been helpin' Aunt Sophie at the hotel and she's been sweet on me fer some time. You know how it is, I have to beat them women off with a stick sometimes," chuckled Mac.

Talon laughed at his friend and said, "Well, I'm happy for you Mac, but I just can't imagine you doin' anything but bein' a Jehu on a stage."

"Well, I been a bullwhacker and Jehu for a lotta years now an' its 'bout time I learned how to handle a rockin' chair an' let a fine woman wait on me. I ain't gittin' no younger ya' know, 'sides, with all this Indian uprisin' it's gittin' to where it's plum unhealthy fer a feller."

The coach topped out and the team stretched to cover the miles across the flats. The trail had previously followed closer to the river and along the flats, but the sandy soil proved too difficult for the teams to make any time and often they had to double-team to get the coaches through.

The new trail led across the flat-top and cut the area often referred to as Alkali flats because of the many areas of the dry white chemical caused by evaporating rains on the dry soil. The dust was rising and filling the coach and when they crossed any alkali, the white dust made the interior even more unbearable.

The passengers tried dropping the dust curtains, but they were of little help and the wind through the door openings brought more dust. The women were busy with one hand fanning at the dust and the other holding handkerchiefs to their nose and mouth. The other passenger was a portly, haberdasher peddler and his restrictive clothing, starched collar, tight waistcoat, and wool suit coat and trousers appeared to be very uncomfortable as he pulled and tugged at his collar and buttons on his waistcoat. Ginny saw his discomfort and said, "Sir, you're obviously uncomfortable. Loosen your collar and jacket, make yourself comfortable. There's no reason not to be."

"Well, I never, I couldn't. I have an image to uphold. I am, after all, a reputable haberdasher," he declared.

Ginny chuckled and said, "Your secret is safe with us, no one will know."

He looked at the young women and twisted on his seat with color rising from his collar to his cheeks. He reached up and carefully took his starched collar off and released the top button on his shirt and exhaled like he hadn't breathed in weeks.

"Oh, my, what a relief. Thank you."

The women smiled and nodded as the coach hit a bump and bounced them closer to one another and the girls giggled at the collision. Johnny was sitting on the center seat and leaning against the door as he held on to the back strap. He was looking out the window when he saw them and hollered to Talon, "Talon! Indians! Over there by them rocks!"

Chapter Twenty-Three

Attack

TALON RELAYED THE alarm to Mac to the response, "Well, unlimber that thar bullwhip boy, we gotta get this team movin'!"

Talon grabbed the blacksnake bullwhip and flipping the coils over his shoulder he brought the length forward against the wind and let the tip crack over the heads of the leaders with the sound of a rifle shot. The horses dropped their heads and put their shoulder into the collars and against the hames to stretch the traces as they lengthened and quickened their stride. With three long strides the team turned the canter into an all-out gallop, The coach rocked back on the thorough braces and the women were pressed against the seat, Johnny clasped the back strap and the peddler almost lost his seat. With three successive cracks of the whip and Mac leaning forward encouraging his team with his "Eeeiiiyaaaah!" Talon coiled his whip and grabbed for the Henry. He turned and leaned over, extending the butt of the Henry to the window and hollered, "Johnny! Give this to Ginny!" and waited for the rifle to be taken from his grasp. When the boy pulled the rifle into the coach, Talon grabbed the butt of his Spencer, withdrew it from the scabbard and readied himself for battle.

Smokey was sheltered by the panniers and saddle Talon had strapped atop the coach and the man now pushed his dog behind Mac and pulled his saddle close behind him. He knew he couldn't use if for a rest, but it would give some protection and help him steady his arm. He looked behind and to the offside of the coach to see the band of Indians, some 10 or 12 warriors strong, lying low on the withers of their mounts and giving chase. Some rose and shook their war lances in a taunting motion as they screamed out their war cries with their heels digging into the ribs of their horses pushing for more speed.

Although well within range of the Spencer, Talon waited for a kill shot and he knew he wouldn't have to exercise his patience too long. The two lead warriors appeared to be in a horse race as they looked at one another as often as they looked to the coach. Talon watched as they whipped their horses with their weapons at hand; one with his bow and the other with a rifle. Talon chose his first target, the one with the rifle, and brought the front sight to bear on the nearing figure. With the jostling of the coach challenging his hold, the young man took a breath and held it, waiting for a steady sight.

An instant later, he recognized his chance and squeezed the trigger. The resulting boom of the Spencer startled the passengers but not as much as the intended target. The near Indian was knocked from his mount as sure as if he had been struck by a charging buffalo. He fell under the mount of his friend and was struck by both hind feet as he tumbled end over end with his blood leaving a trail across the white alkali. The rider of the mount that trampled the first kill almost lost his seat and struggled to regain control of his horse as the others passed him by in their pursuit of the coach.

Talon jacked another round, cocked the hammer and picked a target. Again, the big Spencer roared and the horse of the target dropped his head between his front feet and somersaulted end over tea kettle, throwing his rider face first into the dirt. The rest of the war party was drawing nearer the stage and as Talon was preparing another shot, he heard the Henry bark from below him and saw another Indian take a hit but stay mounted. The Indian grabbed his side, dropping his rifle, and fell to the neck of his horse, reining it away from the horde.

Talon let loose another round and one more attacker was knocked from his horse and trampled under the feet of the other mounts. As Talon started to jack another round, Mac hollered, "Hang on! We're goin' down this hill faster'n we oughta!"

The road dropped off the flat with a quick drop to the ridge-hugging trail that sloped down the face of the bluff. It was steep and challenging on a normal run when the Jehu could start at a walk with his foot on the brake, but Mac took it at a run and pushed on the brake lever as the back end of the coach kicked up gravel and rocked and came within inches of dropping off the edge. He sawed back on the reins and the horses did their best to slow the rig down but it was difficult to stop the momentum of both the team and the coach. "If you ever prayed, do it now!" yelled Mac as he sawed back and forth on the leads.

Talon saw the off-side leader stumble, uttered a quick prayer of help and watched, but with the taut line from the hand of Mac, the big bay was able to regain his footing and didn't fall. The road leveled out and bent away from the side of the bluff.

The narrow roadway stopped the Indians from following knowing; the man with the big gun was a deadly adversary and the narrow roadway would make them an easy target. They huddled together to plan their next action.

Talon hollered to Mac, "They ain't followin' so you can slow down if you're of a mind to." Mac pulled on the reins and let the team slow to a walk and get their breath as he walked them across the dry flat that was about fifty yards away from the river. Johnny stuck his head out the window and hollered to Talon, "Are they gone?"

Talon leaned over and looked at the dusty face of the boy, grinned and said, "Yup, at least for now. Was that Ginny that shot that Indian?"

"Yeah, she kicked me outta my seat and cut loose on him out my winder!"

"Well, you tell her she did mighty fine!"

Johnny dropped back into his seat and grinned at Ginny and said, "Talon said you did mighty fine, Ginny!"

"Well, I was scared to death! I sure hope they're gone for good," she declared as she looked at Mary Sue.

Mary Sue said, "I hope so too, but I'm really hopin' we can wash up when we get to the station. This dust is horrible and I can't hardly breathe."

Ginny looked at her friend and thought how the two of them seemed to be growing apart. Before their capture, they were two giddy girls that enjoyed talking together and laughing about everything. They often spent hours sharing their dreams of family and future and both had talked about home and hearth with similar plans and hopes.

But now, the wilderness seemed to be changing them both. Where Mary Sue was still focused on a home in town with dresses and children and social gatherings, Ginny's thoughts were more about the wilderness, mountains, and facing the challenges of this wonderful country.

Knowing her thoughts had changed, she looked within and realized that Talon had a lot to do with that change and she pictured herself at his side and challenging this wild land. A smile crept across her face as she wistfully looked out the window of the slow-moving coach and Mary Sue asked, "What are you thinking about that's making you smile here in this terrible place?"

"Oh, it's not so bad, except for the Indians, of course. I was just thinking about the mountains and a certain mountain man," she smiled coyly as she looked back at Mary Sue.

145

As Talon searched the entire area for any sign of Indians, he looked along the face of the bluff and marveled at the sandstone and clay formations along the front of the bluff. He noted what appeared to be several caves back in the draws that were sheltered by pillars of clay that were formed by the elements carving away the soft soil below the harder sandstone leaving pillars, humps, and images that could be mistaken for castle turrets or statues. The clay soil crossed the face of the bluff in bands or veins of muted red, yellow and browns. He smiled as he thought of the imagination of the Creator as he formed such images from the soil of the earth. He turned back and asked Mac, "How far is that next station?"

"Fremont's Orchard is just yonder behind that row of trees thar," answered Mac.

"Orchard? There's an orchard there?" asked Talon aghast.

"Nah, but from a distance, them scraggly ol' cottonwoods made ol' Fremont think it looked like an apple orchard, so that's what he called it. But we can take a bit of a break here, course we'll get a fresh team n' all, but Mrs. Wilson puts out a purty good spread fer noonin'."

"Suits me, and I know my horses could use a break after that chase them Indians gave us."

The station at Fremont's Orchard was well built, almost fortress like, with adobe bricks formed in the Sante Fe fashion with adobe, sand, and grasses, dried in the sun and laid up like kiln-fired bricks. A double wall over a foot thick gave the occupants a cool interior in the hot summer days and good insulation for warmth in the winter. A sod covered roof made the structure literally fire proof and the Indians knew any assault on this station would be costlier than it was worth so the Wilson family that ran the station enjoyed their security.

Thomas Wilson and his wife, Edith, enjoyed their work with the station, but he also had several crops that produced a harvest of goods to trade to travelers and added to their comfortable living. His two sons, Dennis, age 14, and David,

146

age 12, had proven to be great helpers and also served as hostlers for the stage line.

When the coach pulled to a stop, the boys immediately set to work removing the harness from the team while Mac and Talon stepped down from the box. Talon looked up at Smokey and clapped his hands to signal the dog to jump in his arms, which Smokey gladly did and almost knocked his master over. He laughed as he let the dog down to the ground to do his customary investigation of the premises. He opened the door for the passengers and helped the ladies step from the coach before Johnny and the peddler stepped down. The peddler was evidently searching for the path to the privy and Mac pointed him in the right direction. Johnny was hot on his heels and they both disappeared around the corner of the station. Tom waved at Mac and said, "Howdy Mac! Who's your new shotgun?" as he walked toward the pair.

"Howdy do, Tom. This hyar's Talon and he ain't all that new. He made a run with me from LaPorte to Big Laramie an' back a while ago," he said as he patted Talon on the back. The young man extended his hand toward Tom Wilson and said, "Pleased to meet you, sir."

"Well, thankee, young man. My, you ain't much older'n my own boys. Just how old are you, young man?" questioned the station keeper.

Before Talon could answer, Mac jumped in with, "He's old 'nuff. He's already saved my bacon more'n onct, yessireee, he done that. Just up thar on the flats just now was one o' them times."

Tom looked at Mac with concern written on his face and replied, "I thought I heard gunfire. What was it, Indians?"

"A whole passel o' them red devils! He got a couple of 'em, an' the young woman in the coach got one too, I think."

"Ya don't say. Well, I think you'll be alright now. They don't come 'round here much. We keep it purty clear far 'nuff out so they ain't got no cover, an' we, that is me'n the boys,

147

can shoot pretty good, so they don't come round here too often."

"From what I hear, ol' Chivington's got 'em riled up sumpin' fierce, so I'd sleep with one eye open, if'n I was you," warned Mac. He rubbed his belly and asked, "So, what's yore woman got fixed for us hungry folk?"

"I think she's got some kinda stew goin' in there. It's smellin' powerful good," he advised.

After everyone was filled and pushed back from the table, Mac motioned to Talon and the two walked out to confer about the road ahead. Mac started with, "I'm thinkin' those red devils'll be waitin' for us when we get back out on the flats an' I ain't too sure 'bout what to do," he spoke as he looked at his Shotgun.

"I was thinkin' 'bout it too. You know the road better'n I do, where do you think they'll try to hit us again?"

"Well, there's a couple a' places, but let's get Tom out here an' see what he thinks." Mac hollered for Tom to join them and the station keeper strolled from the house and walked to their side. "We're thinkin' them Injuns'll try to get us after we leave here. Now, where'bouts long the trail do you think they might hit us?" asked Mac.

Tom dropped his head and shuffled his feet in the dry gravel as he pondered the question. Looking up he said, "There's one place, that if'n I were doin' it, would be the only place to hit a stage." He bent to the dirt and began to draw a semblance of the road and described his thinking to the two men. Jabbing his stick in the ground at a point on the sandy map, he said, "Right there, that's the spot. I'm sure that'd be the best bet."

Talon looked at the men and asked, "What if I rode around and went ahead and set up our own ambush at that site. You think that would work?"

Both men looked at him and at each other and nodding their heads, began to describe the way he would have to go to get around the trail and set up his ambush. "There'll be plenty of cover, an' they won't be lookin' 'cross the river for anything, so I think you could do it. At that place where you'd come up there's plenty of scrub oak and some sage, so you'd have cover. Also, you could see from down below if they're waitin' below the bluff. You just might pull it off," declared Tom enthusiastically.

Talon went to the corral where his Grulla waited and the horse lifted his head expectantly. He was anxious to be under saddle and on their own. Talon saddled up and hung the scabbard for the Spencer under the right fender of the saddle, checked his bags for extra cartridge boxes for the rifle and satisfied, led his horse to the front of the cabin. Ginny was standing on the porch, Henry by her side and looking at Talon, she asked, "You ain't leavin' us are you?"

He grinned at her and said, "No, I'm gonna ride ahead and scout things out a little. I want you to take my place up top just in case Mac has any more trouble. You can do that, can't you?" He pushed his Spencer into the scabbard as he spoke.

She nodded her head and said, "You be careful now, I, uh, we can't be losing you now."

Talon caught her slip of the tongue and smiled as he answered, "Oh, you can't get rid of me that easy. I'll be back directly." He swung aboard and said, "There's a box of ammo sittin' on the seat up there. You do know how to load that thing, don't you?" he said, nodding toward the Henry. She looked down at it, pointed at the end of the muzzle and said, "Well, they come out here, so I s'pose I put 'em in somewhere down yonder," she said with a grin.

Talon tipped his hat and spurred Dusty to move out. Smokey trotted alongside looking up at his master with a sparkle in his eye that told of his excitement to be on the trail again.

Chapter Twenty-Four

Ambush

THE MID-DAY SUN was hot on his back as he gigged his horse into the water to cross the river. Ever-watchful for signs of quicksand, he also scanned the far bank for a route that would provide ample cover through the trees and to the ridge beyond. His plan was to follow the ridge until the cover nearer the river was thick enough to allow him to drop off the ridge and to the tree line. His crossing was easily made and the horse and dog both did their usual shake after the crossing to rid themselves of excess water.

With a simple wave of his hand, he motioned for Smokey to take the trail before them and the dog started out at a trot. He found a game trail that led to the bluff and the dog led the way. Animals usually search out a path that is easy going but also provides protection as they always have some predator higher up the food chain looking for a meal and this path proved to be just what Talon needed.

After cresting the ridge, he moved to the far side and led the way with Smokey now on his heels. Occasionally, he would rein his mount nearer the crest so he could get his bearings and check the landmarks. He watched the course of the river, noting the three islands that Tom spoke of and as the river made a bend back to the west, Talon knew this to be the place to cross.

Before cresting the ridge, he dropped to his feet and with spyglass in hand, he bellied down to search the area below.

He knew Mac would allow just about an hour before leaving the station and Talon knew he was nearing that mark. He scanned the area below and back again before he spotted the group of Indians. They were gathered in a cluster of trees near the edge of the bluff that rose from the river. The horses were at the foot of the bluff and several of the warriors waited while three were standing by some juniper at the top of the edge of the sandstone slope.

Talon watched for a moment, then scanned the area for his route to by-pass the Indians and set up his ambush. As Tom had directed, he saw the trail that would take him through the thicker tree cover and give him a crossing into more trees. He would have to be quick but stealthy about it, and with one more visual check, he returned to his mount.

The tree line provided him with excellent cover and he leaned to the rump of his horse as they slid down the steep ridge. Bottoming out, they moved directly to the riverbank and with another quick glance downstream to see where the Cheyenne were, he was pleased with his cover and started across the water. As he watched for quicksand, he thought about the murky water and was thankful for the runoff that brought the silt. If it had been clear, the Indians downstream would have been alarmed at the muddy water caused by his crossing, but now there was nothing to give him away.

Remembering the map in the sand and recalling that Tom said the roadway was pretty close to the edge of the bluff, Talon knew he would have the cover of scrub oak and sage to set up his ambush. He tethered his horse, withdrew his Spencer and two extra cartridge boxes, and started up the slope with Smokey at his heels. As he neared the top, he bellied down and searched the area for cover and to see if he could locate the Indians. Where he had seen them from the ridge, the bluff that sheltered them would be easily negotiated on horseback and would keep the animals from view of the stagecoach. Talon knew he would probably hear them before he saw them and he searched for suitable cover. A nearby rockpile was partially obscured by some scrub oak and cholla and he rose, stooped to a crouch and made for the spot. He dropped to his knees, lifted his head and looked around at the edge of the bluff where he thought the Indians would come from, back at the roadway and all points around him. He said to himself, *yup, this'll do.* He quickly found a comfortable position that allowed him to fire from the cover of the oak brush, but not reveal himself. The rock pile would give some protection and he had a clear view of the roadway.

He was no sooner settled than he saw the team and coach crest the roadway coming up from the bottom. That would be where the Jehu would slow the team to a walk and let them have a breather before whipping them up to a canter for the remainder of the trip. It was then Talon heard the sounds of horses coming through the brush off to his left and just below the crest of the slight bluff and he knew the Cheyenne were preparing their attack.

Mac slapped the lines on the rumps of his team and they picked up their step to a canter as the Indians burst from the tree line shouting and screaming as they kicked their horses to cut off the team at Mac's hands. Instead of swerving or stopping, Mac slapped them again and shouted his "Heeeeeyaaaahhh!" and the horses jumped to a gallop surprising the Indians.

The attackers quickly kicked their horses to an all-out run to pursue the stage and Talon heard the bark of the Henry. He dropped the blade of his sight on the warrior in the lead and with his elbow on his knee for a steady aim, squeezed off a shot. The Spencer's blast startled the Indians, but the bullets impact; the bullet to the chest of their leader that knocked him from his mount and dropped him on his back beneath the hooves of the horses, surprised them more.

Several turned to locate this new threat and while they searched for the source, Talon revealed himself with the roar of the Spencer that took its toll on a second attacker. He jacked another round and quickly found a target. Before the Indians could change their tactic, a third Indian, with half his head missing, was knocked from his horse. Before the smoke cleared, Talon heard the bark of the Henry and saw another Indian knocked sideways off his mount and under the feet of a nearby pony. The war party had numbered twelve before their first attack and now only five remained. Their leaders gone, the rest reined up and skedaddled. The coach had passed Talon's location, but Ginny told Mac, "They're leavin,' hold up for Talon!"

Mac sawed back on the lines and when the horses dropped to a walk, the grizzled old man searched around and viewed the dust cloud of the disappearing attackers. Then he saw Talon standing and watching. He pulled the coach to a stop and waited for Talon to join them. After tying off his mount, the Shotgun threw his saddle and gear atop the coach and climbed up to the box. Ginny had seated herself beside Smokey and had her feet on the seat between the men. When Talon sat back she rested her hand on his shoulder and said, "Glad to see you made it back. I was beginning to worry about you there for a while."

He turned to look at her and smiled and said, "You just try to keep me away, girl." She smiled back and squeezed his shoulder as Mac slapped the leads to start the team on their way. They didn't expect any more trouble from the Cheyenne knowing the Indians were usually quick to cut their losses and regroup before trying another attack. They put high regard on retrieving their dead and returning them to the families for grieving.

Talon knew the Cheyenne would return to the place of the conflict and retrieve the bodies of their dead brothers and would take the time to return to their village before gathering a band of warriors to make another attack on whatever they deemed a good target on which to vent their wrath and gain plunder.

"I shore was glad to hear your thunder when you cut down on them red devils!" said Mac as he worked the team. "I was hopin' you wouldn't be too fer away, but Ginny here, she done a good job, too. I'd hire her any day to be my Shotgun!"

Ginny grinned at Mac knowing that was high praise coming from an old-timer. She cradled the Henry in her arms and said to Talon, "You might have a hard time gettin' this away from me, I'm kinda likin' it!" as she looked down at the brass mounted rifle.

"Uh, that's a gift from my Pa, but we can look around and maybe find one for you," he answered.

Ginny smiled at the thought of them looking around together to buy a rifle. She knew her future was uncertain and that her family had probably gone on with the wagon train to find a home in Oregon, but she thought maybe staying here in Colorado territory and being near Talon was what she wanted. She knew they were both young, but she knew of other young people that got married at the same age they were and had made a go of it, and if others could, it might work for them.

Her face flushed with her quiet thoughts and she was glad she sat behind Talon, so he couldn't see her blush. She took a deep breath and looked around at the scenery. It was still flatland, but there was more variety with buttes, ridges, more vegetation and greenery along the river bottom. Occasionally, a jack rabbit would catch her attention or a circling hawk and she was pleased with knowing that everywhere she looked there was life. *This is good country, and the closer we get to the mountains, the better I like it,* she thought.

Ginny turned and lay back against the saddle and pushed up the saddle blanket to make herself more comfortable. With Smokey curled up in front of her, she soon drifted off to sleep with the rocking and swaying of the coach. Mac looked over his shoulder at the girl and elbowed his partner causing Talon to look back at the serene scene and smile. Mac said softly, "Ain't too many women can curl up fer a nap after an Injun attack. She's a keeper, son."

Talon chuckled as he cast a sidelong glance at the would-be cupid sawing at the lines for the team. There were sixteen miles between the stations of Fremont's Orchard and Eagle's Nest and because of the delay at the Orchard, it was mid-afternoon before they drew within sight of Eagle's Nest. When Mac saw the trail of smoke rising from the location of the station, he pulled back on the leads and with his foot on the brake, brought the coach to a stop. The horses pranced nervously as the men looked quietly and carefully at the blackened remains that sat smoking almost a hundred yards farther along the roadway. Talon slipped his Spencer from the scabbard and stood on the seat to look around. Johnny called from his window, "What's wrong? Why are we stopped?"

"Hush boy, be quiet now," hissed Talon without taking his eyes from the station. As he surveyed the area he let his eyes linger on two clusters of juniper and pinion on the far side of the station, the ravine beyond, and the few cottonwoods that stood near the smoldering remains of the cabin. Beyond the cabin, there was more left of the barn, but only enough to identify it as having once been a barn.

The poles from the corral were scattered and askew. There were no horses or any other living thing within sight. "Go ahead Mac, move on closer," instructed Talon, still searching the area for any sign of danger. Smokey was on his feet, looking around and Ginny stirred awake. When she saw Talon standing with one foot on the forward edge of the boot and the Spencer held ready, she knew there was something amiss. She sat up and held the Henry ready and also looked at the remains of the station. The coach moved closer and the horses showed their discomfort as they began to prance sideways and look back and forth with their eyes wide and their teeth showing as they pulled at the bits.

Mac pulled the coach to a stop, tied off the leads to the brake lever and moved to get down from the boot. He always had a shotgun in the boot and reached back for it as he stepped down. He cocked both hammers on the double-barreled coach gun and walked toward the ruins in search of the station keeper and the hostler.

He saw the charred remains of the keeper just past the door sill where he lay with the barrel of his burnt rifle beside him. Mac continued to look around and stepped back from the smell of burnt flesh and looked to Talon as the young man walked toward the barn. Talon stopped as he saw the mutilated remains of the hostler lying alongside the poles of the corral. He turned and said to Mac, "Here's the hostler, did you find anyone?"

"Yeah, the keeper's there in the cabin. That's all they had here, just the keeper and the hostler. It was just a stop for a change of teams, no meals or nuthin'," replied Mac. He turned to the coach and said over his shoulder, "I'm gonna undo the horses and take 'em to water. You take care of your'n and let the passengers stretch their legs."

Talon returned to the coach and told Ginny to let the others out and that he would take the horses to water and let them get a little graze. "We're gonna have to rest here a spell so the horses can cool off and get some graze, cuz we're gonna have to keep goin' and they ain't used to that."

Ginny nodded her head and started to the coach while Talon tended to his horses. Johnny followed Talon to the water's edge while he watered his horses and staked them out so they could get some graze. Mac had tied off the leaders of the team and was on his way back for the swing pair. Talon let his eyes continually rove the area and any places of cover that might hide an attacker. He was certain whoever attacked the station was long gone with the stolen horses and didn't believe there was any danger, but he remained cautious.

Johnny walked beside his friend as Talon started for the wheelers, or the last pair of horses in the team. As he started to undo the harnesses, he handed the big Spencer to Johnny and said, "Can you hold on to this for me?"

The boy grinned widely and said, "Sure can!" as he reached for the big rifle. Talon knew this stop would be for at least an hour to give the horses ample rest before starting on to Latham.

Chapter Twenty-Five

Reprisal

THE SOD STRUCTURE WASN'T much more than a hut. Part dug out, part sod building, sod roof, the soddy fronted the corral that was put together with stacked stone for posts and twisted cedar for poles. Two horses, ribs showing and heads hanging, stood hip shot in the muddy corral waiting and hoping for some grass that rarely came.

Behind the corral stood a buckboard that hadn't moved in several months. Whiskey Sam Raymer ran what he called a trading post that catered to Indians and the occasional wandering settler. Located at the junction of Wild Horse Creek and Pawnee Creek and in the middle of buffalo country, most of the settlers were either lost or looking for some place to hide. Whiskey Sam was happy to relieve them of any burden that hindered their travel, like money, whiskey or other gear. Indians would bring in coyote pelts and buffalo robes to trade for rusty trade fusils or whiskey or some odd gee-gaws, beads or other trinkets. Every fall, Whiskey Sam loaded up the pelts and robes and trekked to Latham or Julesburg and trade them for other goods.

When Two Bears stood in the door there wasn't much light that shone around him. Although not exceptionally large, the Indian filled the small doorway. With only one window on the south side of the dug-out, the room was filled with shadows and dark corners.

Whiskey Sam asked his visitor, "So, ya got sumpin' to trade, do ya?"

Two Bears stepped into the room and lay two Sharps buffalo rifles on the counter. Sam looked up at the Indian with surprise registered on his face and asked, "So, where'd ya git these?"

Two Bears grunted and said, "Trade for those," pointing to a rack behind Sam that held two Hawken rifles. Two Bears was familiar with the Hawken and knew how to load and fire them, but the breech loading Sharps required ammo that Two Bears didn't have. He could, however, use the Hawken with black powder and ball. Sam looked back at the Hawken and knew one Sharps was worth two Hawken and this Indian wanted to trade two Sharps. He smiled at his good fortune and turned back to the Indian with a somber expression and said, "I dunno, I don't have bullets for these," shaking his head.

"I want those two and that one," pointing at a Paterson Colt hanging on a couple of pegs beside the Hawkens.

Sam looked to see what Two Bears was pointing at and shook his head, "Nah, I can't do that. But, I'll give you one Hawken and plenty o' powder and lead for it so you can shoot all you want. I'll even throw in a jug o' whiskey!" he declared. Sam lifted one of the Sharps to test the heft and action while he waited for Two Bears to agree. He added, "And that's my last bottle of whiskey, your friends just traded me outta the others."

Two Bears looked at the man and asked, "Friends?"

"Yeah, there were two of 'em, traded me some robes and a couple a' coyote pelts for a couple jugs of whiskey. Don't think they made it too fer though, they was drinkin' purty heavy when they left. Probly' down in the draw yonder-passed out."

"Trade," said Two Bears to show Sam he agreed to the trade.

Sam nodded his head and reached behind him for the jug of whiskey. From the shelves to his right he took two cans of black powder, two bars of galena lead and a bullet mold. He turned to Two Bears and asked, "Which one do ya want?" pointing to the Hawkens.

Two Bears pointed to one and Sam retrieved it for him and placed the Sharps on the rack. He turned around and saw Two Bears walking out the door with his trade goods in hand. He watched as the Indian put the powder, lead and mold in a parfleche on his pony then swing aboard with whiskey jug in hand. The Indian left in the direction of the draw indicated by the trader looking for the other two Indians.

The draw was a shallow arroyo that was carved by spring rain runoff and now held nothing but a sandy bottom and cactus laden banks, but the two men were seated on the shady side of the bottom with their horses searching for anything edible. They argued over the single jug that was held by the bigger of the two and were startled when Two Bears appeared at the edge of the dry bank. He looked at the two men, recognized them as Cheyenne but did not know them and asked, "What village are you from?"

The larger of the two stood and staggered to gain his footing, looked at Two Bears and said, "We don't have a village, the blue coats destroyed it."

"Why did they not kill you?" asked Two Bears.

"We were gone on a hunt and came back to find nothing but death."

Two Bears dropped from his mount and said, "I am Two Bears," and placed the jug on the ground, and walked closer to the men. "We should hunt together, and we should hunt blue coats and white men."

The big man said, "I am Buffalo Hump and this is my friend, Black Elk. Join us and we will drink together."

"Let us eat and decide what we should do. Save your whiskey for later," said Two Bears as he dug in his parfleche for a handful of jerky.

It was soon evident to Two Bears that these men had been wandering aimlessly and were now trying to drown their grief. He learned that the village, though small, had included the family of Buffalo Hump and the woman of Black Elk. Both men were proven warriors but their village chief, Little Bear, had tried to make peace and forbade his men to fight against the white man and the blue coats. Now they were all dead and these men, like Two Bears, wanted vengeance. When Two Bears suggested a raid on a stage station to steal supplies and weapons and to get vengeance against the white man, both Buffalo Hump and Black Elk readily agreed.

When Two Bears had fled from the ranch and his embarrassing experience with the Sharps, he waited and watched as those he had attacked left the ranch. But now there were three men and a boy, and he was but one warrior. He knew they were traveling in the direction of the stage road by the Platte River and he hoped he might one day catch up to them and have his vengeance. Now with the two additional warriors with him, perhaps he would gain from a reprisal raid and find these men and destroy them.

Two Bears was familiar with the stage road and the many stations, having traded at some and watched others as they were built. Most of the Cheyenne thought the white men foolish to have so many horses and so few men, but when they saw the stages they understood. But they also saw the stations as a source for horses and other plunder. Now Two Bears thought of the different stations and settled on one that he thought would be easier to take than the others. After his experience on the stage line and the Virginia Dale station, he wanted one that didn't have as many people to fight. He knew the station at Eagle's Point only had two men and now that he had additional warriors, that would be a good place to get more horses and weapons. With more weapons and horses he could recruit more warriors to join his own Dog Soldier band and then he could fulfill his purpose as a great war leader and chief of the Cheyenne.

It was late on the second day when the three bellied down on the small bluff behind the Eagle's Nest station. When Two Bears pointed out that only two men were there and yet eight horses were in the corral, the warriors grinned and Buffalo Hump said, "This will be easy to kill two white men and steal horses and maybe weapons. You are right, Two Bears, we will do as you say."

The slight draw with the pinions and cedars provided enough cover for the two warriors to get near the station. Two Bears had followed the draw to the cluster of juniper and pinion and hidden from view of the cabin, he stealthily approached the barn. When the hostler emerged with a pitchfork of hay, he was met with Two Bear's tomahawk.

Buffalo Hump and Black Elk ran from the draw toward the cabin and rounding the corner of the building came face to face with the station keeper with a rifle held at his hip. The keeper fired into the chest of Buffalo Hump but Black Elk fired his fusil, hitting the keeper in the chest and knocking him back into the cabin. Black Elk screamed his war cry and followed the keeper into the cabin and plunged his knife into the white man's neck; drew it to the side, almost decapitating him as the blood spewed out and splattered on the chest of Black Elk. The Indian screamed again, "Aaiiieeee," and scalped the man.

Two Bears came to the doorway, saw Buffalo Hump lying in a puddle of blood and looked to see Black Elk scalping the white man. His face split with his malevolent grin and stepped over the body to see what prizes awaited. The keeper had fallen on his rifle, breaking the stock to the dismay of his killer, but the warriors gathered other plunder by way of powder, lead, sugar, beans and a few other staples. As he started to leave, Two Bears smashed a lantern on the body of the white man and using the cinder shovel from the stove, scooped some hot coals from the stove and lit the cabin on fire. He carried the remaining coals to the barn and threw them in the hay causing the barn to be quickly consumed in flames.

Two Bears kicked the poles from the corral and shouted to send the horses running, knowing he and Black Elk could gather them later. He stood and looked around for any other plunder and seeing none, raised his Hawken above his head and shouted his war cry in defiance of the white man, thinking this was just the beginning of his reprisal raids.

Chapter Twenty-Six

Revenge

THE TWO WARRIORS WERE belly down and behind a clump of sage as they watched through tufts of buffalo grass. After spending most of the morning rounding up the herd of horses and corralling them in the distant arroyo with brush and driftwood from the dry creek bottom, they heard the rattle of trace chains and the clatter of hooves that told of an arriving stage. They saw the cloud of dust chasing the stage and quickly hid below the ridge of the small bluff at the edge of the arroyo.

As they watched the driver and shotgun on the stage search the area and unharness the horses, they began to consider another attack but were stayed when they saw there were a total of five men and a boy. Even the boy carried a rifle. They decided to wait until the stage left then take their horses and leave the area. Two Bears continued his vigil while Black Elk checked the horses. Since the horses were far enough away and out of sight of the stage team they knew there was no danger of alarm, but Two Bears watched and waited.

With the team and the other horses tethered at the river, Talon and Mac started digging a couple of graves for the keeper and hostler. Johnny sat nearby with the Spencer across his lap while he watched the men at work with the spades from the remains of the barn. There wasn't much left of the keeper, but the hostler's body was already starting to swell and stink and caused the men to stop digging with only a shallow hole before them. When they sat down on the pile of dirt to take a breather, Johnny lay the Spencer by the stone he used for a seat and told Talon, "I'm gonna go talk to my sister an' see if she's got anything to eat."

Talon nodded his understanding and watched the boy go toward the stage where Ginny and Mary Sue sat on a log that had been used for a bench at some time in the past. The drummer was perched with his rump on the step of the coach and fanning himself with his brown derby.

Mary Sue said to Ginny, "That ol' sun is gettin' hot!" as she shaded her eyes and looked up at the afternoon sun. Ginny looked as well and grabbed her hat, releasing her hair and shaking the long locks to get some air. Mary Sue copied her and dropped her head to run her fingers through her hair and tossed her hair back and said, "That feels better, that hat was gettin' hot!"

Two Bears was startled when he saw the first one remove her hat and show the long hair, but when he saw the red hair he realized who they were. Two women, one with red hair, and a boy, his captives! That would mean the man digging the grave was the one that killed his warriors and the one that took the women from him. This was his time for vengeance. The spirits were with him and his medicine was good. Rage began to simmer in his gut and he turned to Black Elk, "Look, those are not men. They are women and they were my captives. He is the one that I will kill to get my vengeance!" pointing at Talon.

"But there are two other men and that young warrior had a rifle too," responded Black Elk as he looked toward the station compound.

"No, the fat one at the stage has no weapon. The other one is an old man and the boy no longer has a weapon. We will kill them all and have many more horses and their weapons. Then we can get more warriors and show the Cheyenne how weak these white men are and we can kill many bluecoats. You can have vengeance on the bluecoats that killed your woman, and I will have vengeance on the white man that took my captives. I will make him watch while I kill them and then I will cut him open and watch him die," snarled Two Bears.

The Indians waited until Talon and Mac grabbed the body of the hostler; Talon at his shoulders and Mac at his feet, before they charged. In his rage, Two Bears screamed his war cry and it was just enough of a warning for Talon and Mac to drop the corpse and try for their weapons. Black Elk charged at Mac with his tomahawk raised and stumbled on the dirt pile but still hit Mac with his shoulder, knocking him down. The Indian, having hit the jug after rounding up the horses, staggered into the grave and was crawling out when Mac rolled over and scrambled toward his coach gun.

At the same moment Black Elk struck Mac, Two Bears charged at Talon. But Talon, realizing he couldn't make it to the Spencer, reached for his Remington pistol and was drawing it when the tomahawk of Two Bears struck down, hitting the pistol barrel, and knocking it from Talon's grip.

When Two Bears pulled back with the hawk, Talon followed it with his balled-up fist and struck the Indian in his windpipe, knocking him back. Talon snatched his own tomahawk from his belt and charged after Two Bears. The Indian stepped aside and tripped Talon who fell face- first and lost his grip on the hawk, but quickly rolled over to avoid the downswing of the Indian's hawk, which struck the ground just inches from his head.

Talon brought his right fist into the side of the Indian and heard a rib crack as the Indian grunted and rolled off but started scrambling to his feet. Talon also gained his feet and the two men began to circle one another as Talon reached behind his head and brought out his Bowie knife.

As the two men did the circle dance of death, Talon heard the discharge of Mac's coach gun and hoped the old man was alright, but Talon had to focus on his own problem. With the Indian trying a feint, Talon sidestepped and scored with his knife, drawing blood across the Indian's wrist.

Two Bears acted like he didn't even notice and Talon continued to watch his eyes as he felt for his footing while both men in their crouch sought an advantage. Talon feinted to his right and when Two Bears dodged the knife, Talon struck him with a wicked left to his side where Talon had heard another rib break. The Indian winced and grabbed at his side, but stepped back to avoid another swing.

He acted like he was hurt and Talon sought to press his advantage and lunged forward, but Two Bears stepped aside just enough to allow him to bring his hawk down on Talon's shoulder. The buckskins he wore protected Talon so the blow was a glancing one, but Talon stumbled and started to fall.

Two Bears stretched out his leg and tripped the young man, causing Talon to sprawl forward on his face. He quickly rolled to the side but Two Bears was on him and the men grappled like wrestlers in an ancient Olympic arena. Talon was on his back and Two Bears straddled him but while Two Bears held Talon's wrist, rendering his knife useless, Talon held Two Bear's wrist; the hand that held his Tomahawk.

The test of strength was going to Two Bears with his weight astraddle Talon and the young man was beginning to think he was going to lose this contest. The image of Ginny and Mary Sue crossed his mind, but he was weakening. His injury was on the shoulder that had been wounded earlier; the same one Two Bears had struck so violently. Now it was

167

giving away and Two Bears felt the give in the young man's strength.

The Indian surprised Talon when he pulled back, resulting in wrenching his hand with the tomahawk free. He raised his arm and started to scream his war cry when suddenly, a rifle barrel was thrust in his face and Ginny snarled to the Indian, "Remember me?" and pulled the trigger.

The blast of powder from the Henry blackened the Indian's face and even though he started to pull away, the light of recognition was chased away as the bullet pierced his eye socket and blasted out the back half of his skull, splattering blood and detritus of bone and hair across the pile of dirt by the grave. The Indian's body slumped onto Talon's chest, who quickly squirmed out from under the bloody mess.

He looked at Ginny and she grinned back as she stepped up to him and wrapped her arms around him. She laid her head on his chest, heaving a deep breath and leaned against him. Talon slowly wrapped his arms around her then had a thought. Looking around, he saw Mac sitting spread- legged on the ground and holding his coach gun across his lap. A pile of blood and bone lay about eight feet before him and Talon easily read the sign of the blood trail.

Apparently, Mac reached the coach gun before the Indian had reached Mac and the Jehu made sure he wouldn't, when he pulled both triggers and blasted the Indian into several small pieces. Mac sat with his head hanging and his chest heaving, then looked at Talon and grinned. He struggled to his feet, walked to the graves and said, "Whadaya think we ourta do wit' 'dem?" motioning toward the Indians remains.

Talon looked around and said, "Nuthin'." Looking up, he saw several turkey buzzards circling and said, ". . . we'll just let the clean-up crew handle this mess."

They finished their grave detail, returned to the horses and led them back for harnessing. It was just a short while before they were ready to start the last leg of the day's journey. Knowing it would be dark when they arrived in Latham, they still figured the danger of an attack that close to the settlement was less than if they tried to stay at Eagle's Nest. They had just pulled out of the compound and hadn't stretched out the team, when Talon said, "Whoa up," as he looked past a clump of juniper and towards a ravine. "Look yonder, there's the horses from the station. Maybe we oughta let 'em outta there, whatcha think?"

"Yup, reckon so, they ain't got water, else I'd say leave 'em be. But if you kick down the barrier, they'll probly just make their way back to the station. I'll tell 'em in Latham what to look fer. Go 'head an' set 'em loose. I'll wait right chere fer ya. Be sure ta take your big gun," he warned. Talon cradled his rifle and walked to the gulley, saw no sign of a threat and kicked down the brush barrier to make way for the horses. He didn't try to spook them out, knowing they would find their own way free when they got thirsty and started looking for water.

Talon climbed back up to the box and was surprised to see Ginny had reclaimed her seat on top and within reach of Talon. Smokey sat beside her with his head on her leg as he watched his master seat himself. Talon rubbed the dog's head and looked at Ginny and asked, "Just whose dog is he anyway?"

"Ours," she smiled in reply.

Chapter Twenty-Seven

Latham

THE SETTLEMENT OF LATHAM was at a crossroads of the East – West Overland Trail and the spur line to Denver City. At the confluence of the Cache La Poudre river and the South Platte, the fertile valley drew settlers to farming and ranching. When the gold rush of 1859 brought wagon trains full of gold seekers, several families settled in the Latham area while the men went searching for Gold along the front range of the Rockies.

With Latham being a hub of traffic for settlers, farmers and gold seekers, and now the Overland Stage route, it was a growing community with several new businesses along the main street. The usual number of saloons and gambling halls crowded the smaller businesses like the corner café, the women's dressmaker and millinery shop, the men's haberdasher, the general store and the undertaker. But new false-fronted buildings were going up and the community was looking forward to having a church and a school.

The Overland Stage station was on the west end of the main street with a livery stable on one side and a hotel with a restaurant on the other. The glow of lanterns within was a welcome site as Mac leaned back with leads in hand to bring the stage to a stop directly in front of the station. Smokey was standing alert and fought for balance as the coach rocked to a stop. Ginny had her arm around the dog as she looked the town over. There wasn't much to see in the dim light of early night, but her broad smile told of relief and happiness at their safe arrival.

Talon stood to stretch his long legs with one foot on the edge of the boot and a hand at the side rail of the box seat. Looking around he said, "Well, I don't see any Indians, so I guess it's safe to get down," as he turned to grin at Ginny. She playfully slapped him on the shoulder and replied, "Didn't you see that one we passed back yonder? Maybe he's just playin' possum and waitin' to take your hair!"

Mac climbed down on one side and Talon the other. The young man reached up to catch Smokey as he jumped from up top and putting the dog to the ground, he reached to help Ginny as she stepped from the box to the step to the hub and down to the ground. She fell against Talon and he thought it was no accident, but he didn't mind as she wrapped her arms around him as he caught her. "Oh, excuse me sir. You are such a strong man and you saved me from falling, you're my hero!" she declared with a giggle, feigning the way of a fainting woman.

"Well, miss, maybe you need me to escort you to your room?" kidded Talon.

"Well, I never, you are entirely too bold and we just met!" she continued with her pretense as she fanned herself looking every bit the offended female.

"Will you two quit fawning over each other and help a lady down!" said Mary Sue from the door of the coach. The two released each other and Talon turned to help Mary Sue from the stage. Johnny hopped down without using the step and stood with hands on hips as he looked around the town. There was little to see with the only light coming from lanterns near the windows of the few businesses and most of them, saloons.

"Haruummph, I say there, young Talon; before I leave I want to thank you for what you've done in providing us with a safe journey. I'll not be going on west, my journey will be to Denver City, so I wanted to thank you before parting," said the drummer as he extended his pudgy hand to shake with Talon.

"Thank you, sir," responded Talon as he shook hands with the man, "and I hope you have a safe journey the rest of the way."

He watched as the peddler made his way into the station. The hostlers were busy with the team and another worker was removing the luggage from the boot. Since the women didn't have luggage, Talon walked with them to the hotel next door. Mac had explained to Talon about the arrangement the stage line had with the hotel and he knew there would be rooms available for them.

As they entered, they were surprised at the well-appointed interior of the hotel. A large chandelier hung in the center of the open foyer and their attention was immediately taken by a tall counter with a matronly woman seated on a stool behind it.

She greeted them with a broad smile and said, "My, my, my, I bet you ladies would like a bath, wouldn't you?" The two friends looked at each other and realized how they must appear in their men's duds and layers of road dust and laughed as they turned to the woman. Mary Sue replied, "I'm not sure one bath will do, it might take several soakings to find us! But yes, we would love to have a bath!"

"Fine, fine, we'll just let the men take care of getting the rooms and let us go to the bath rooms," said the woman as she reached out her hand to guide the women away. Talon wasn't sure the woman had even seen him and Johnny, but he chuckled as he watched them leave. The woman turned and called over her shoulder, "Michael, Michael! Take care of the desk!"

Talon had turned to watch the women leave and was surprised when a voice behind him said, "May I help you?" Talon turned back around to see a young man about his same age standing behind the counter and waiting.

"Uh, yeah, the stage line said you kept rooms available for passengers and such and those two ladies, and their brother here, need a room."

"Yessir, we can do that. And I see my mother has taken them for a bath but we will have a room for them waiting. Is there any luggage for the ladies?"

"Uh, no, and about that. Ya see, these ladies lost everything in an Indian raid and they need some clothes. Is there any way we can get them some dresses and such right away? I mean so they'll have some clothes when they get outta the baths back there?" asked Talon.

"Hmmm, I think we might be able to help with that. My aunt Mabel has the ladies store just down the street and she's lives upstairs so, I think we can get the ladies something. Before we go, will you be staying with us as well?"

"Yeah, an' I might even get one o' them baths too. I been on the trail for a while and I'm probly' a little gamey myself and the squirt here, too," said Talon as he nudged Johnny. The clerk jotted something down on the ledger and closed the big book before coming from behind the counter. "Come with me, then," he instructed.

Talon and Johnny followed the young man as he went from the hotel, crossed the street and walked down the boardwalk past the Gold Crown saloon and knocked on the door of the ladies' shop. A woman's voice called out, "Who is it?" to be answered by the young clerk with "It's me, Aunt Mabel, I have some customers for you. Can you help us?"

They heard footsteps and the shade on the windowed door rose revealing a spitting image of the matronly hotel-keeper. She opened the door and said, "I thought you said you had some customers for me, these are men and I don't have men's clothes!" she said, very annoyed.

"It's not for them, Aunt Mabel, it's for two women that came in on the stage. They lost everything in an Indian raid and they need some clothes."

"Oh, well, all right then. Let's see what we can do," then looking at Talon she said, "Is one of these ladies your wife?"

"No ma'am, one of the women is this boy's sister and the other is her friend. I'm just helping them out."

"Well, how am I going to get paid?" she asked before moving any further in the shop.

"I will pay you, will gold coin be alright?" asked Talon. The woman's countenance immediately changed and she said, "Yes, yes, of course. Now, what size are the ladies and what all do they need?"

"Uh, well, I don't rightly know their size, they're 'bout the same size I reckon," he started as he looked at Johnny, who shook his head in agreement, and he continued, ". . . about this high," holding his hand about shoulder high, "and, well, uh, you know, not skinny but not plump either, uh, well, you know, about right."

"Men! You don't have any idea, do you?"

"Well, how 'bout this, how 'bout you just gatherin' up what you think they'll need and bring it over to the hotel and put it in their rooms for them to put on, and that'll be fine," he stated with embarrassment showing and his eagerness to leave evident. He reached into his pocket and pulled out two twenty dollar gold pieces and handed them to the woman and asked, "Will that take care of everything?"

"Oh, yes sir, certainly sir. I'll take care of that right away."

"Now nothin' real fancy, I mean, not like those women in the saloons, cuz these are ladies, now. Just somethin' nice, you know, kinda like what you're wearin',"

"Of course, I'll take care of everything," she responded dismissively.

Talon looked at Johnny and said, "Let's go to the general store, maybe we can find you some duds too."

"Does that mean I gotta take a bath too?" grumbled Johnny as Talon tousled his hair.

"Yup, we both gotta take a bath cuz, as we are, we ain't fit comp'ny for the women. They won't wanna be around us, smellin' like we are."

Johnny sniffed at his shirt and said, "I don't smell nuthin'!"

The owner of the general store was closing his door to turn the open/closed sign around when Talon caught the edge of the door and asked, "Could we just get a few things, some clothes for the boy, before you close up?"

The man looked at the pair and said, "Sure, c'mon in. We'll get you fixed up." He stepped back as he opened the door, let the two young men in and called out to his wife, "Fox, we've got a couple fellas need some clothes. Can you help them while I finish closin' up?"

A woman came from behind the counter and Talon noticed she was Indian. He glanced back at the store keeper and at the woman, then said, "We just need something for the boy."

"Right over here," she motioned to a table top loaded with men's trousers and shirts. She looked at Johnny and said, "Would you rather have buckskins like your Pa?"

"Yeah!" he declared enthusiastically, ". . .but he's not my pa," he mumbled with his head hanging. The woman looked at Talon and asked, "I do have some buckskins that would fit him if you want," as she looked at the buckskin attire of Talon. She reached to touch Talon's shirt, noticed the patch repair from when he was wounded, and added, "I also have a shirt that would fit you," then she added as she looked at his shirt, "Arapaho?"

"Yeah, my Ma made it, though she's not Arapaho, but she was raised by 'em."

"I am Ute, of the band of Walkara in the Sierra Madre," she replied.

Talon grinned and chuckled before replying, "Then you know Spotted Owl?" The woman smiled and said, "Yes, she is the daughter of our chief. But how do you know her?"

"She married a friend of mine and they're now part of my family's ranch. Her husband is Reuben but your people had another name for him, I think."

Lame Fox grinned at Talon and said, "It is good to know a friend of our people."

In a short while, Talon and Johnny stood at the counter preparing to pay for their new clothes when Talon noticed a gun rack behind the counter and a familiar rifle standing at the end of the rack. He asked Lame Fox, "Is that a Henry there on the end?" She turned to look at the rifle he was pointing to and answered, "I think so, but my husband will have to help you with that," she said as she motioned her husband to join them.

"Yessir, that's the first Henry we've gotten in; ain't she a beaut?" he asked as he handed the rifle to Talon. The young man looked the rifle over, dropped the lever to look at the chamber and asked, "Do you have a couple of boxes of ammo to go with it?"

The storekeeper grinned and said, "Now, that's a pretty expensive rifle, are you sure you want it?" Talon nodded with a wide grin and said, "I've already got one, well sorta, but to get it back I need this one to replace it, you know how women are."

The storekeeper looked confused, shook his head and tallied up the bill. He grinned broadly as Talon paid in gold coin, quickly wrapped the buckskins up for Johnny and watched as the pair left his store.

Chapter Twenty-Eight

Refreshed

THE HOTEL KEEPER, MARGARET, was made privy to the surprise gifts of dresses when her sister, Mabel, and her son, Michael, carried the parcels into the lobby of the hotel. With wide eyes she said to her son, "Well, I wondered where you disappeared to, what is all this?"

"That fella that was with those two you took to the baths asked Aunt Mabel to fix them up with some new clothes, so here we are!"

"My, my, my, well let's take them up to their rooms," she said as she grabbed the extra key from behind her and started to the stairway.

"I'm sure those two will be in the baths for a while yet, so we'll just lay things out on the bed," she instructed.

Mabel answered, "I'm going to wait for them because the dresses might need a touch of altering or something."

They busied themselves laying things out for the women with two dresses and assorted accessories for each one, Michael had to make an extra trip for the rest of the trappings. They were no sooner finished than the two girls, wrapped in

177

blankets, came into the room and stood with surprised looks on their faces. Ginny said, "I'm sorry, I thought you said this was our room," as she looked around at all the items displayed on the beds.

Margaret said, "It is, dear, it is. These are from the young man you were with and this is my sister, Mabel. She owns the dress shop and she's here to make sure these are suitable for you both. Also, my son informed me that the young man will be waiting for you in the restaurant downstairs when you are ready."

There was an abundance of chattering and giggling between the four women as the girls tried on dresses and accessories. Margaret dismissed herself while Mabel tended the fitting and adjusting but the hotel keeper returned with hairbrushes, combs and hand mirrors. She helped both ladies with their hair and in a surprisingly short while, both Mary Sue and Ginny were totally transformed.

Talon and Johnny made short work of their baths and grooming and were seated near the doorway into the restaurant when a muffled giggle caught Talon's attention. He turned to see the two ladies that held no resemblance to the trousers wearing, dusty faced pair he left at the hotel lobby. Mary Sue's dress was of a deep green and brown plaid with a fitted bodice and a small white collar. Full puffed sleeves had a lace cuff and the broad ruffle of the full skirt was topped with matching lace. She smiled broadly as she stepped forward, revealing Ginny in her brown and tan silk taffeta dress with a pattern of wide brown horizontal stripes that accented the lighter tan and floral pattern. The sleeves were highlighted with a contrasting band of floral ribbon applique at the cuff that matched the edge of the wide lace collar. Her fitted bodice was offset with a narrow brown belt sporting a gold buckle at the front. Both women showed color rising from their neckline as they stepped to the table.

A breathless Talon stood, motioned for Johnny to stand, and pulled out the chairs on either side for the ladies to be

seated. The women noticed the buckskins on Johnny and Mary Sue said, "Well, look at you, little brother. Aren't you the real frontiersman in buckskins?"
Johnny smiled as he ran his hands down the leather sleeves and flipped the fringe as he said, "Yup, just like Talon!"

Their eyes went to Talon, who had put on the set of buckskins he had in his packs that were new and had more decorative beading. With fringe at the sleeves, yoke and legs, his movements were accented as he seated himself. The broad bands of beading that went over both shoulders, held a floral pattern in shades of blue on a white background and outlined with porcupine quills. The yoke had a row of white elk's teeth just above the fringe and accentuated the broad shoulders of the young man. The four took a few moments looking at each other and simultaneously broke out in laughter as they were quickly reminded how different they now appeared than just a few hours earlier.

It was the first time the four had been able to enjoy a meal together. The days of the previous weeks had been so jammed full of staying alive and getting back to the settlements, the idea of enjoying a sit-down meal in a nice restaurant was the furthest thing from their minds.

They savored both the meal and the time together. Thick slices of roast beef nestled against a pile of potatoes and carrots, smothered with savory gravy and set off with heavily buttered fresh sourdough bread was a meal to enjoy, and enjoy it they did. The ladies were careful with their etiquette but Johnny and Talon were not so inclined and the two young men wasted little effort as they downed the scrumptious meal.

They sat back and looked at their clean plates and Talon said, "I think I'll see if the kitchen might have some scraps for Smokey, he's probly' wonderin' what happened to me. Course, he's keepin' Mac and Dusty comp'ny at the station so I think he'll be alright."

"If you'll wait till we're finished, we'll walk over there with you. It'll be nice to get some fresh air, don't you think, Mary Sue?" said Ginny, looking from Talon to Mary Sue.

"Oh, why don't you two go ahead, I think I'll just go up to our room."

"Uh, Mary Sue, I'd sure like you to come with us, there's somethin' I been meanin' to talk to you about," said Talon, obviously uncomfortable.

"What is it? Can't we talk about it here?" she asked with concern written on her face. She was thinking it was going to be about him and Ginny and she let a smile tug at the corners of her mouth, "Or is it something you two want to share privately?"

Talon looked from Mary Sue to Ginny and realized what she was implying and stuttered, "Oh no, it's nothin' like that, but it would be better away from all these folks," he said as he motioned toward the other diners. She nodded her head in understanding, smiled at Ginny and the ladies were soon finished with their meal. Talon settled the bill and the four started their evening stroll with Talon carrying a paper bundled package of scraps for Smokey.

As soon as they exited the hotel, Talon started with, "I know you've been anxious to get to LaPorte and to see your Ma, but . . ." he hesitated and cleared his throat, "Mac told me the doctor said he did all he could, but," and he paused to consider his words, "your Ma didn't make it."

"What do you mean?" asked Mary Sue as they stopped on the boardwalk.

Talon had spotted a pair of rocking chairs in front of the hotel and directed the women in that direction as he said, "Mary Sue, I'm sorry, but your Ma has passed."

She looked at Talon with a blank stare and when Johnny asked, "You mean our Ma died?" she looked at her brother and pulled him to her side. Another step took her to the chair and she dropped into the rocker as Ginny pulled the other chair near to her side.

Ginny took her hand and said, "Oh, Mary Sue, I'm so sorry." Johnny leaned his head on his sister's shoulder and she put her hand to his cheek as they touched foreheads and she whispered, "It's just you and me now, Johnny."

Talon dropped to one knee in front of the women and took Ginny's left hand and Mary Sue's right and he said to them, "Look, we've been together a lot these last few days, and as far as I'm concerned, we're family. So, don't you go thinking it's just the two of you. I've been giving it some thought and I know things are gonna work out for all of us. We'll just stick together and I'm certain the good Lord is going to take care of everything."

As Talon watched, the women and Johnny had a good cry together but soon started wiping at tears and looked to the man before them. Mary Sue said, "So, Talon, just what are you going to do with two women and a boy? We can't be living together, it's not proper."

"Well, I been thinkin' 'bout that too. Mac an' me have worked out a deal for a cabin he's got up on the Cache La Poudre, just a little ways from LaPorte. He thinks it'll make a right fine home, so . . ." he let the thought hang, knowing there would be a few details to work out, but at least it was a start.

He knew he had steady work with the stage line and he wouldn't be around too much so the women would have it all to themselves, and Johnny of course, but there was nothing improper about that. At least they would have a home to call their own until something else could be provided and from what Mac said the cabin should be more than suitable.

He left the girls to their talking and rocking and took Johnny with him to the station to give Smokey his scraps and talk to Mac. When they returned, Smokey was at his heels with tail wagging and eyes happy to see Ginny.

The women smiled at Talon and Johnny and Mary Sue said, "Well, we're agreed. We'll see what kind of home that cabin will make and see about getting a job in LaPorte when we get there."

She looked at Johnny and back at Talon and saw the boy looking up at the man. She suddenly knew her brother had found a new father figure and she was glad for him. They *did* look somewhat alike, both in buckskins and moccasins. She felt Talon would be a good influence on her brother and a great help to her and Ginny. She also knew Ginny was thinking more on the romantic side of things concerning the broad-shouldered young man.

"Did you show her yet?" asked Johnny as he looked up at Talon.

"Show me what?" asked Ginny as the boy looked at her.

"I couldn't Johnny, it's up in the room," explained Talon.

"All right, what are you two up to now?" asked Mary Sue.

"Well, I guess it's time for all of us to turn in anyway, so you can stop by our room and I'll show you," explained Talon.

Johnny rushed into the room before the others and stood beside the bed with a broad grin on his face as he watched the others enter. Talon let the ladies go before him and when they were inside, he walked to the bed and threw back the blanket to reveal the Henry.

He looked at the women with a smile and they looked back with a question on their face as Ginny said, "So, that's your Henry, but what were you going to show me?"

"That's *your* Henry, and those boxes there are shells for it."

She looked at the rifle and back at Talon and said, "You can't give me that, you said your Pa gave you that as a gift."

"No, that's a different one. I bought that for you so I could get mine back," he said, grinning broadly.

She walked over to the bed, picked up the rifle and held it close as she examined it. She looked at Talon and said, "Now all I need is a set of buckskins and I'll fit right in."

Talon grinned as he thought about the conversation he'd had with Lame Fox when he asked her to make a set for Ginny.

The Ute woman told him she had a set that was probably the right size and almost finished, and a few hours work with beads would make the top complete and he could pick them up in the morning. Johnny wasn't near enough to hear the conversation so Talon was certain it would be a complete surprise.

He thought Ginny would want a set and now that she said as much, he was feeling pretty pleased with his decision. As he thought about it all, he agreed with Mac as he thought, *Yeah, she's a keeper alright.*

Chapter Twenty-Nine

Cache La Poudre

THE STAGE FROM LATHAM to LaPorte had to wait for the stage coach on the spur from Denver to connect before leaving. It was mid-morning when the spur wagon arrived, and with no passengers on this particular run, the Jehu chose to bring a mud wagon with a four-up hitch to haul the several bags of mail.

With the LaPorte bound coach waiting, it took just a few moments to transfer the bags from the wagon to the boot of the coach and Mac was soon climbing aboard to start the run. Talon was seated on the bench seat in the box and Smokey was standing on top with his head near Talon's shoulder. Mac grinned as he finagled his way to his seat and let out a groan as he settled in and reached to the brake lever to grab the lines. "Well son, this hyar little jaunt should be easy goin' 'less you try to skeer up some Injuns just to keep things int'restin'," drawled the old-timer.

He cackled his usual laugh and slapped the reins to the rumps of the horses to start off then as an afterthought leaned around and hollered to the passengers while the stage rocked forward, "All aboard! We're pullin' out!" He looked over at

Talon and said, "Hope them wimmins and boy made it, I'd hate to leave 'em behind!"

"Oh, we got 'em all, don't worry 'bout that. They've been sittin' in the coach just chompin' at the bit to get started," chuckled Talon.

They cleared Latham and were on the trail on the North side of the Cache La Poudre river as they started across the rolling flats toward their destination of LaPorte. This would be the last leg of the trip driven by Mac and ridden by Talon; as their relief was waiting to take over for the north and west leg of the long Overland Trail that would take them to Fort Bridger.

Talon was feeling good as he could see the mountains within reach and the plains receding behind him. His Grulla and pack horse were again tethered behind and followed on a long lead and Talon was growing anxious to be off the coach and back on his horse heading for the high lonesome.

His thoughts began to swirl around the image of Ginny and he smiled as he remembered the way she felt in his arms and how she looked up at him with her wide, dark brown eyes. When he'd left home just a few weeks ago, he was feeling melancholy and a bit heartbroken with his twin brother, Tyrell, winning the affections of their childhood friend, Elizabeth. Part of the reason he'd left the Medicine Bow ranch was to be free of what he thought was a loss when Elizabeth proclaimed her choice to be Tyrell.

And now he was already thinking about a life with Ginny, a woman he hardly knew, but it felt so right. Everything about her just seemed to fit his idea of a life mate. She wasn't afraid to pick up a rifle and stand beside him to fight anything that came their way, and she was pretty too. He began to think about his Ma and Pa and how young they were when they were married and the life they now had together.

He also thought about how everything could be taken away in just a few moments and wondered if it would be fair for him to even consider taking a wife when the whole country was in such a turmoil. Everybody was saying the war couldn't last much longer and maybe things would be better, but the Indians sure didn't see it that way. With the attacks the Cheyenne made on the stations and the things the soldiers had done in retaliation, would there ever be peace on the frontier?

Mac was watching Talon and could tell he was struggling with something so the wizened old codger asked, "So, what's troublin' ya, son? You're lookin' purty perplexed. Wanna talk about it?"

Talon looked at the Jehu and shook his head as he started, "Mac, I just dunno. You said you're gonna get hitched with your woman from the hotel and goin' back to St. Louie, but what's wrong with stayin' here?"

"Ain't nuthin' wrong with it, but St. Louie is her home and she wants to go back. I spent some time thar when I was a younker like you an' I ain't much fer the city, but she's got a big ol' house back thar n' some family, so, I think I can put up with it. Cain't you just see me a sittin' on the porch in a rockin' chair and lettin' her wait on me in my old age?" he cackled at the thought himself.

"But, if you were younger, and she didn't want to go back to the city, would you still get married? I mean with all the Indian stuff and such goin' on?"

Mac looked sideways at the young man and said, "Uhhhumm, I git it. You're wonderin' if'n you should get hitched with that little gal ridin' back thar, ain'tchu?"

Talon nodded and grunted a "Mebbe, I dunno."

"Wal youngin', the way I see it, whenever and wherever you are when ol' cupid slings his arrows atcha, ya' oughta just be happy yore gettin' a chance fer sumpin' special. Thar ain't no guarantees 'bout nuthin' in this hyar life, an thar's a lotta folks never get the chance to start a family. Just think 'bout all them sojer boys that went off to that durn war back east. Don'tchu think they'd a whole lot druther be thinkin' 'bout gettin' married to a purty little gal like that Ginny, than to be layin' face down in the mud with all their dreams gone? You darn tootin' they would! And it don't make no never mind how old you are or aren't neither. I seen the way she looks at you and vicey versy, so if'n you think you oughta, then don't waste no time doin' it. You might not get 'nother chance!" declared Mac.

Talon looked at him and grinned, nodding his head in agreement and felt like a big weight had been lifted from his shoulders. He reached back and rubbed Smokey behind the ears and said to the dog, "I know you want to keep her around, don't you boy?" Mac laughed at the young man talking to his dog and slapped the lines to the horses to make better time.

The canter of the horses rocked the coach and Ginny looked out the side windows to admire the scenery of the clear stream and the mountains beyond. This was the same route the wagon train had followed before the girls had been captured. Ginny remembered the first time she saw Talon on the boardwalk in front of the general store in LaPorte and smiled as she recalled the brief and even blunt conversation that passed between them. She also remembered looking back to see Talon watching them with a grin on his face as she and Mary Sue continued on the boardwalk and spoke to one another about the good looking young man they'd just seen.

Mary Sue saw the smile and asked, "Are you thinking about him again?"

Ginny turned to face her friend and said, "Yes, I can't help it. It seems like no matter what I look at, I see him, and no matter what I think about, he's in my thoughts."

"I think it's love, it must be, because you're not the same Ginny I grew up with and talked about boys and dreams and everything with. You've changed."

"Is that bad?" asked Ginny, concerned.

Mary Sue giggled and said, "Of course not, silly. I'm happy for you. I just hope I'm as lucky as you and find me a man soon. But I'm not sure I want to stay out here with all the Indians and stuff. Maybe I could find a husband that would

want to go to the city, you know, maybe St. Louis or New
Orleans, or someplace like that."

"Oh you! You're always telling me about God having a
plan for your life, don't you think God can have a plan for you
out here in the west? Maybe He'll take you to Denver City!
They say that's going to be a big city someday. Or what about
Golden City? They say that might be the new capital city of the
territory. Or . . ."

But, before she could name another town, Mary Sue
interrupted with, "Honestly, I just want to find the man God
has for me and make a home with children and be happy. If
it's here, then so be it," she said with a firm nod of her head.

She turned to look squarely at Ginny and whispered, "Do
you really think you and Talon will get married?" with a
conspiratorial grin and peeked at Johnny to see if he was
paying any attention to their conversation. The boy was fast
asleep and stretched out on the opposite bench at the front of
the coach. "I dunno, but I'm thinkin' that's what I want. I
never thought I'd be thinking about marriage now, what with
everything that's happened, but I think it just made things
clearer for me. Especially after Talon told me about being a
Christian and we prayed together. I dunno, it's just been
different. Things like a life together with someone you love
and friends and things like that, they're just more important
than before. I really believe God has used this experience, such
as it was, for His purpose and He, God I mean, means much
more to me now."

Mary Sue looked at her friend and took her hand in her
own and said, "That's wonderful Ginny, just wonderful."

As Mac sawed back and forth on the lines, Talon asked,
"So, is this your last trip? Are you and your woman... what is
her name, anyway?"

"Her name is Minnie. Ain't that purty, just 'bout as purty
as she is, and yes, this is my last trip. When we get to LaPorte,
I'm climbin' off and turnin' it over. And I tell you what, I been
meanin' to tell you, youngin'... You know I went for weeks

an' I dunno how many runs an' never had any Injun trouble till you come along! That's right," he said shaking his whiskery head, "nary a one, 'till we run up against them red devils at Virginia Dale an' ever since then, whenever you been sittin' right thar it seems like ever Injun in the territory's out to lift yore hair. Why, after you left after them wimmin, I didn't see nary a redskin till I picked you up agin, and we hadn't gone fer atall, an' here they come a screamin' an' a hollerin' and burnin' stations an' such. I'm beginnin' to think yore one o' them magnet things, you know, them things that attract stuff. That's it! Yore an' Injun magnet!" he declared and cackled at his own joke.

The women noticed a change in the roll of the wagon and looked out the window to see the road pulling away from the river and more trees along the roadway and hillsides. The terrain looked more familiar and they realized they were nearing the town of LaPorte. They watched from the windows as the coach pulled into town and came to a stop in front of the station.

Mary Sue remembered, somewhat wistfully, that she had expected to see her Mother here and the thought brought a tear to her eye that she quickly dabbed away. Both women took a deep breath and turned to the door to step into this new chapter of their lives.

Chapter Thirty

Home

AS MAC STEPPED DOWN from the driver's box, Talon watched as the old man walked beside the team and rested his hands on the necks of the horses and spoke to each one. It was evident the whiskery Jehu was saying goodbye to the horses and to his decades as the driver of the coach. Mac looked up at the front boot and the driver's box, sighed and then turned to see Talon watching.

Mac grinned, dropped his head and stepped to the rail that Talon leaned on to watch the solitary walk around of the old man. With a broad grin Mac said, "Say, young'un, how 'bout you and the ladies joinin' me fer lunch o'er at the hotel. I'll introduce you to my woman, Minnie, and I'll even buy y'alls lunch. How 'bout it?"

"Mac, I think that'd be just fine. I'm sure the ladies would enjoy a good meal at Aunt Sophie's, and I'm pretty certain they wouldn't pass up the opportunity to meet Minnie."

"Alrighty then, I'm headin' o'er there now, so when you get 'em all gathered up, just you come on," invited Mac. Talon nodded his head and turned to enter the station and let the ladies know of the invite. They were chattering away with the station keeper's wife and when told about the invitation to Aunt Sophie's, they gladly accepted and were ready to leave.

When they entered the restaurant, they spotted Mac sitting alone at a big round table in the corner and visiting with a woman standing by his side. When he saw Talon and the women, he grinned and waved them over to the table. Mac stood and proudly introduced his intended, Minnie, with, "Folks, this is my Minnie. She's the woman that is the sun of my life and my reason to retire!"

The entire group smiled broadly and introduced themselves in turn, and expressed their congratulations to the pair. When they were seated, Minnie took their order and went to the kitchen. Mac said, "Ain't she sumpin'? I still can't believe she wants to spend the rest of her life with this old codger, but I ain't lookin' a gift horse in the mouth. I'm just gonna count my blessin's and enjoy it."

"Well, Mac, I think you deserve to have her in your life and to enjoy your time together. It ain't often that an ornery ol' coot like you gets that lucky, so you better enjoy it!" kidded Talon.

Mac laughed and nodded his head in agreement then turned serious as he said, "You know sumpin,' young'un? I was just thinkin' that you said the ladies here were gonna be lookin' for a job, and I'm takin' Minnie away from this job, mebbe Sophie would be willin' to take one or both of these girls on to fill Minnie's shoes," declared Mac, grinning at his own idea.

Talon looked at Mary Sue and Ginny with a questioning expression and raised eyebrows to see their response. The two women looked at one another, nodded their heads and Mary Sue said, "That might just be the answer for us. Is she around so we can speak to her about it?"

"I'll have Minnie put in a good word fer ya' and then we'll see 'bout talkin' to her," answered Mac.

By the time they finished their meal, Minnie had spoken to Aunt Sophie and the woman had visited with the women at the table and agreed that Mac's idea was a good one. She said she could put both ladies to work right away and would also provide a room at the hotel for them to stay while they worked. She said, "With Mac here taking away my best worker, that means her room will also be available, so you ladies might as well take it. That way you'll be handy to work and not have to worry about the extra expense of some other place to live."

After Sophie left the table and the group was ready to leave, Talon asked the women if they still wanted to see the cabin and they both readily agreed.

Ginny said, "Yes, we want to see it, after all, it might be our new home and when we're not at the hotel, it would be nice to have a place to get away," she declared. She was really thinking that her hopes were to have this as her home with Talon and not to have to be at the hotel. But she knew Talon might be hesitant to make that commitment right away, and she was willing to give him time. She had come to believe she loved him and hoped he felt the same about her, but they were both young and this might not be the right time. As Talon turned to open the door for them, she looked at his back and thought, *but I hope we don't have to wait too long.*

Mac followed them out and now he knelt at the edge of the boardwalk and drew a map in the dirt to give them directions to the cabin. Talon watched and questioned until he was certain he could find his way and with a glance at the ladies he said, "I'll be right back. I'm goin' to the livery and get us a wagon or buggy to take us out there."

They agreed and began a leisurely stroll along the boardwalk as they waited for his return. They walked the length of the business district and crossed to the other side, heading back in the direction of the hotel and station. It was just past mid-day and the bright sun was warm on their faces and they enjoyed the peacefulness of the town and their walk.

They stopped in front of the woman's millinery and looked at the hats and bonnets on display, discussed what they liked and didn't like, and resumed their walk. The line of people that extended out of the general store reminded the ladies of their first walk down this street a few weeks ago, when they'd first met Talon.

They had to step from the boardwalk and into the street to bypass the crowd and were just approaching the walk again when two men staggered from the Four Aces saloon and bumped into the women. One of the men fell to the walk and cursed at the ladies as they tried to get away. He grabbed out and caught Ginny's foot and tried to drag her down but she kicked herself free and Mary Sue grabbed her arm to pull her away from the men. Some of the crowd saw the ruckus but no one came to the aid of the ladies as the two men, both now standing, tried to grab them and tore Ginny's dress in the process.

"Wal, quit pullin' away from me, woman! C'mere and let me give you a kiss," he slobbered. His friend laughed and looked at Mary Sue, reached for her, missed, and stumbled against the building.

"Get away from us, and leave us alone. You're drunk!" declared Ginny as she held the shoulder of her dress and tried to step back from the men. The first drunk grabbed at her again and hollered, "I said c'mere! You think yore too good fer us?"

"She is too good for you and if you touch her again I'll introduce you to the devil himself!" snarled Talon as he stepped up behind them. Both men whirled on him and the first one laughed as he said, "Why, yore just a pup! You ain't worth my time. Now, go on home to yore momma, boy, and let the men take care of these here women!"

Talon made a slight feint of a turn away from the man, dropped his shoulder and brought a balled-up fist from the ground up into the stomach of the boaster, doubling him over with a loud expulsion of stinking breath as he fell forward on his face, tumbling from the boardwalk to the street with his face landing in a pile of fresh horse apples.

Talon then turned to watch the second man who reached for his pistol but his wrist was struck by the flat side of Talon's tomahawk causing the man to drop his weapon and grab at his hand, now numbed from the blow.

He looked at Talon and saw a man with blood in his eyes making him back up and quickly looking around for a way of escape, he made a staggering run down the boardwalk to flee from the scene.

Talon stepped to the street and seeing the first man still unconscious, nudged him with his foot to roll him to his side so he wouldn't suffocate with his face in the horse droppings. The crowd watched and spoke among themselves, but refused to leave their place in line to give any assistance to the three young people. Talon looked up at Ginny and Mary Sue and said, "Are you ladies ready to go?"

They nodded and without saying anything, climbed into the two-seater buggy where Johnny waited and settled into the back seat for the ride to the cabin. While they rode, Mary Sue helped Ginny make a repair to her dress so the she wouldn't have to keep holding it and when that was done, they sat back to enjoy the scenery.

As he handled the team, Talon thought about what had just happened and the way he felt when another man was confronting the women. He had never felt such sudden rage and fear when he thought Ginny was threatened. He didn't take time to think, he just reacted, because someone he cared about was endangered. He had stepped forward and helped others before and he knew he would have done the same thing even if he didn't know the women involved, but he also knew the way he felt this time was different. Just the idea of another man even presuming that he could have his way with Ginny was disturbing to him and he knew he could not allow anything to separate him from her again.

Just a short distance from town Talon looked to his right to see the first landmark Mac had spoken of. It was a big hog-back that looked like a giant table top that angled up, exposing layers of granite beneath that now formed a jagged cliff that overlooked the town. The road followed the Cache La Poudre River as it flowed from the canyon of the same name.

The stream, that could barely be called a river, was usually less than ten yards wide and not over knee deep. But the water was crystal clear and chattered and chuckled as it danced over the rocks to make its escape from the granite-walled canyon. The countryside was green with the new growth of early summer and with the over-arching blue of a cloudless sky, the beautiful day became memory-making as they made the leisurely drive to the cabin.

The stream twisted its way toward the valley with a variety of tree-lined banks. Cottonwood, Aspen and Ponderosa Pine cast their shadows away from the mountainside that was covered with jagged boulders and random cedar and pinions. It was a tranquil scene and an inviting one as they neared the cutoff to the cabin.

As the main road bent to the west in its pursuit of the creek, the cutoff took a route that skirted a grassy shoulder that extended a couple hundred yards from the timbered slope rising to the granite-topped mountainside.

As they rounded the bend of the road, the cabin came into view and Talon stopped the buggy to give everyone a long look at the peaceful scene. The cozy log cabin was tucked into the edge of a cluster of Ponderosa and Fir that skirted a cliff wall that seemed to hold back the mountains. Talon slapped the reins on the rumps of the team and they started off as the road bent around the grassy slope and worked its way to the front of the cabin. Larger than most settler's cabins, the log structure had a peaked roof covered with split cedar shingles and the roof line extended over the wide porch along the front of the building. A door stood in the center with four-paned windows on either side. A ladder back rocking chair sat idle but inviting anyone to sit and enjoy the serenity.

When Talon stopped the buggy, no one hesitated to climb down and step into the cabin. The ladies entered first and were surprised to find a well-kept home. Since they'd expected a tawdry bachelor's retreat, they were amazed to see curtained windows, an orderly sideboard with dishes and pans, a well-crafted table with four chairs and a broad fireplace with all the hardware necessary for hanging a pot for good, warm meals. Opposite the fireplace but nearer the counters was a small but sturdy stove that would be suitable for cooking. The girls walked slowly around, touching everything and were amazed there wasn't a thick layer of dust. Everything seemed to be clean and tidy. Talon opened the side door that led to a sizable bedroom that held a brass bed adorned with a colorful quilt.

"My, this would make a nice home," said Mary Sue as she continued looking around. "Everything is so neat and clean, surely Mac had some help taking care of this."

"He said it belonged to a couple that wanted to try to raise horses but after their first year, they thought the winters were too much for them and they went back to New Orleans," said Talon.

"I can't imagine anyone wanting to leave a home like this, I think it's beautiful!" said Ginny as she pulled at the shoulder of her dress and fussed at it a little. Talon noticed her discomfort and said, "Just a minute, I'll be right back."

When he returned, he handed Ginny a package and said, "You might wanna go in there," nodding toward the bedroom, "and see if it fits, or even if you want 'em."

She looked at Talon and asked, "What is it?"

"Just go on in there and find out," he suggested.

She nodded to Mary Sue to join her and the two disappeared into the bedroom. The squeals of delight from Ginny escaped the bedroom and Talon and Johnny smiled at her response. Mary Sue came out first and Ginny followed, looking down and touching the new buckskins and giggling.

She looked up at Talon and said, "Does this mean I get to be a part of the mountain man club that you two belong to?" as she looked from Talon to Johnny.

"Maybe, but maybe we oughta talk about it first. Come on out to the porch for a minute," he said as he extended his hand to her. She followed Talon out the door while Mary Sue put her arm around Johnny and held him back with her.

Talon looked at Ginny and smiled, dropped his head and struggled a bit as he started, "Ginny, I've been thinking, and I think we oughta be gettin' married. I mean, I know we haven't known each other very long, but I've never felt this way before and as near as I can figger it, I'm pretty sure I'm in love with you. I can't bear to think about you bein' with another man, like when those two were tryin' to, you know, earlier in town. It just made me boilin' mad and I couldn't stand the thought of not having you with me."

Ginny smiled and listened, doing nothing to ease his struggling with what he wanted to say, but waited patiently. When he paused, she asked, "Are you asking me to marry you?"

"Uh, yeah, ain't that what I said?" he replied, confused.

"Well, where's the ring?"

"Ring? What ring?" he asked looking as if he was afraid he had done something wrong.

"You know, when a man asks a woman to marry him, he's supposed to have a ring to give her. I don't know if I can marry a man that can't even give me a ring," she said solemnly.

Talon looked at her astonished at what she was saying and in his exasperation replied, "Ring! Good night, woman, I bought you two new dresses, a Henry repeating rifle, a new set of buckskins, a horse of your own, and now a cabin for our home and you won't marry me because you don't have a ring?" he asked.

She laughed and said, "You bought me a horse?" and watched as he nodded his head. "Oh Talon, of course I'll marry you," and jumped into his arms, knocking him down but she went down with him and landed on top of him, kissing him all over his face. He grinned and wrapped his arms around her and hugged her tight.

Johnny and Mary Sue ran out of the cabin when they heard the crash of their falling and seeing the two with Talon flat of his back on the porch and Ginny still kissing him, they laughed and clapped in happiness at the two lovebirds who refused to be interrupted. On the return trip, Ginny moved Johnny to the back seat with his sister and she sat beside her intended and rode the rest of the way with her arm through his and leaning her head on his shoulder.

Talon sent word to the ranch and asked his folks to come for the wedding. He was pleased when Caleb and Clancy, together with Tyrell and Elizabeth, were present when the small group of friends and family gathered at the cabin for the circuit riding preacher to perform the ceremony of marriage for Talon and Ginny.

Mac and Minnie were there as well as Aunt Sophie. Mary Sue and Johnny were to be a part of the ceremony and were waiting in the cabin for it all to begin. It was a surprise to most everyone present, when it actually became a double ceremony with Tyrell and Elizabeth joining in the occasion to make Caleb and Clancy doubly proud and happy.

After the exchanging of vows and the customary kisses, everyone gathered together for the big feast prepared by Aunt Sophie and Minnie. While everyone was enjoying the food and their time together, Clancy leaned over to Caleb and said, "I never thought I'd see this day and be so happy about it. Now, I'm afraid these two are going to make us grandparents long before we're ready!"

About the Author

Born and raised in Colorado into a family of ranchers and cowboys, B.N. is the youngest of seven sons. Juggling bull riding, skiing, and high school, graduation was a launching pad for a hitch in the Army Paratroopers. After the army, he finished his college education in Springfield, MO, and together with his wife and growing family, entered the ministry as a Baptist preacher.

Together, B.N. and Dawn raised four girls that are now married and have made them proud grandparents. With many years as a successful pastor and educator, he retired from the ministry and followed in the footsteps of his entrepreneurial father and started a successful insurance agency, which is now in the hands of his trusted nephew. He has also been a successful audiobook narrator and has recorded many books for several award-winning authors. Now finally realizing his life-long dream, B.N. has turned his efforts to writing a variety of books, from children's picture books and young adult adventure books, to the historical fiction and western genres which are his first love

Discover more great titles by B. N. Rundell and Wolfpack Publishing at:
http://wolfpackpublishing.com/b-n-rundell/

Made in the USA
Columbia, SC
20 December 2020

29074634R00115